Holiday Royale

Christine Rimmer

D0032689

HARLEQUIN® SPECIAL EDITION®

Recycling programs
for this product may
not exist in your area.

ISBN-13: 978-0-373-65782-7

HOLIDAY ROYALE

Copyright © 2013 by Christine Rimmer

Printed in U.S.A.

"Oh, Damien. I really am sorry I dragged you out of bed, but I've been working up the nerve to approach you concerning a certain, um, issue, for weeks now."

One look at Lucy Cordell's fresh face had Damien wishing he'd put something on under his robe. Still, he was very fond of Lucy. He led her into his suite as she blushed and said, "Thank you, Dami. You're always so kind to me." All at once her big eyes brimmed with moisture.

"Luce?" He jumped up, went around to her and knelt by her chair, taking care as he did it that the damn robe didn't gape and embarrass them both. "What is this? Tears? Now dry your eyes and tell me what's been troubling you."

Lucy hesitated. "Oh, Dami. I've been out of the mainstream for so long. But not anymore. I'm well and I'm strong and I'm living my dream. And I really need to get started on doing the things that healthy women do—"

Dami made another stab at finding out where all this was going. "So you came to me for advice then?" He reached for his coffee cup.

And Lucy said, "No. Not advice. Sex."

He set the cup down sharply. "Say again?"

"Dami, it's so simple. I want you to be my first."

THE BRAVO ROYALES:
When it comes to love, Bravos rule!

Dear Reader,

Lucy Cordell has spent most of her life in and out of hospitals. Sickly and frail, she missed out on all the things others girls enjoy while growing up. But two years ago, she had the surgery that finally fixed her faulty heart valve. She's healthy and strong now, and she's determined to live the rest of her life to the fullest. She's moved to New York City and will be starting fashion school in the spring. Hungry for all that life has to offer her, Lucy needs a special holiday favor from a good friend.

Damien Bravo-Calabretti, Prince of Montedoro, is the darling of the tabloids. They call him the Player Prince and there's always a new, gorgeous woman on his arm. He's smooth and sophisticated and oh-so-charming. He adores Lucy—but in a completely nonromantic, best-friends sort of way. He would do just about anything she asked of him and in the past, he's come to her rescue in a big way.

But then she approaches him with an extraordinary request. To help her, in this case, seems impossible. Then again, Lucy is one determined young woman.

And in the magic and wonder of the holiday season, well, who knows what might happen? The Player Prince just might begin to see sweet Lucy in a whole new light.

Wishing you and yours all the joys of the season,

Christine

Books by Christine Rimmer

CHRISTINE RIMMER

came to her profession the long way around. Before settling down to write about the magic of romance, she'd been everything from an actress to a salesclerk to a waitress. Now that she's finally found work that suits her perfectly, she insists she never had a problem keeping a job—she was merely gaining "life experience" for her future as a novelist. Christine is grateful not only for the joy she finds in writing, but for what waits when the day's work is through: a man she loves who loves her right back, and the privilege of watching their children grow and change day to day. She lives with her family in Oregon. Visit Christine at www.christinerimmer.com.

For my sons,
Matt and Jess.
Happy holidays
and all my love.

Chapter One

At eight-thirty on Thanksgiving morning, Damien Bravo-Calabretti, Prince of Montedoro, heard a knock on the outer door of his palace apartment.

Damien had given his man, Edgar, the holiday off. That left the prince to ignore his uninvited, way-too-early visitor—or get out of bed and answer the door himself.

He was quite comfortable in his bed, thank you. Paying no attention to the continued tapping seemed the most attractive option.

But the knocking continued.

And then he thought, *Vesuvia?*

And that had him glaring at the coffered ceiling far above his bed. *Not V. Please.* It was much too early to have to deal with V.

Besides, it was over between them. She knew that as well as he did.

Not to mention she was supposed to be in Italy, wasn't she? And there were guards at every entrance. She couldn't just stroll in uninvited. How could she have gained access to his rooms, anyway?

Who knew? A man never did when it came to V.

And if it *was* V, he could forget drifting back to sleep. She would keep right on knocking until he gave in and answered. The woman was nothing short of relentless.

Muttering a few choice expletives under his breath, Dami shoved back the covers and grabbed his robe. He shrugged it on and belted it as he strode down the hall.

By the time he reached the door that led out into the palace corridor, he was angrier than he should have allowed himself to be. He yanked the door wide with a scowl on his face, prepared to tell the impossible woman on the other side exactly what he thought of her.

But it wasn't Vesuvia after all. It was sweet little Lucy Cordell, whose brother, Noah, would be marrying Damien's sister Alice in the spring.

At the sight of his less-than-welcoming expression, Lucy's pink cheeks flushed red and she jumped back with a soft cry. "Oh! It's too early, isn't it? You weren't even up...." She gave him a dazed once-over, from his bare feet to the section of naked chest displayed where the robe gaped a bit, and upward. She took in the dark stubble on his jaw and his uncombed hair.

Dami instantly felt nothing short of sheepish. He straightened the robe and raked a hand back through his hair. "Luce. Hullo."

"Go ahead, say it. Too early, I knew it."

"No. Really. It's fine. Not too early at all." If he'd known it was Lucy, he'd have put something on under the robe. Dami was very fond of Lucy. She was so fresh scrubbed and sincere—charming, too. And she did look fetching this morning, all big brown eyes and short tousled hair, and a smart and imaginative ensemble she had no doubt created herself. He could almost forgive her for dragging him from his bed.

She was not soothed by his assurances, but instead winced and scrunched up her pretty face. "Yikes! I get it. You've got company, right?" And then she was off and chattering. "Oh, Dami. I'm sorry, truly. I don't want to interrupt anything, but I've been working up the nerve to approach you concerning a certain, er, issue, for weeks now."

"Working up the nerve?" He gazed at her, bemused. "What issue?"

"Ugh. I hate myself."

He gestured her into the suite. "Come in. We'll talk."

"But you're *busy....*"

"No, I'm not. And I promise you, I am completely alone."

"Really?"

"Truly. Now come in."

But she only sighed and covered her eyes with her hands and then spread her fingers enough to peek out at him. "This is so awkward and weird, isn't it? But I just, well, this morning, I finally couldn't stand it anymore."

He stepped to the side and waved her in again. "Whatever it is, let's not discuss it out here in the hallway. You must come in. We'll have coffee."

She didn't budge, except to drop her hands away from her face and wrap her arms around her. "I just *had* to see you. And so I decided to go for it, before I lost my nerve, you know? But of course, I see I should've at least waited until nine or...later or whenever you... Oh, my Lord." She let her head fall back and groaned at the carved painted ceiling overhead. "You would think

I had no manners at all." She looked at him again, her gamine face crumpled in misery. "Oh, Dami. Sorry, sorry. This is awful, isn't it?"

"Luce, what *are* you on about?"

She blinked at him again, her mouth trembling. "You know what? I'll just come back later and maybe then we can…"

The flood of words stopped when he caught her hand. She stared up at him, her mouth slightly agape in a confused expression that he found simultaneously humorous and captivating. "Come inside now." He gave her fingers a tug.

"Oh, I just don't…"

"Luce." He snared her darting gaze and held it.

"Oh, God." Her plump cheeks puffed out with a hard breath. "What?"

"Come in. Please."

That did it. Finally. She gave him a sad little nod. And then, slim shoulders drooping, she let him draw her over the threshold.

Pausing only to shut and lock the door, he led her down the hallway, past the sitting room and his bedroom, the dining room and his small study. At the back of the apartment, he had a narrow galley kitchen for those times when he preferred to dine in private. He led Lucy to the small table by the one window at the end and pulled out a chair. "Have a seat."

She dropped to the chair cushion, folded her hands neatly in her lap and didn't utter a word as he got to work grinding the coffee beans, filling the French press and setting it on the cooker to brew. He would have preferred, while they waited for the coffee, to run back down the hall and throw on something more appropriate than his black silk robe.

But he was afraid if he left her alone, she just might bolt. He couldn't allow that. Clearly, she did have something to say to him. It was all very intriguing. He wasn't letting her go until she revealed what had brought her to his door.

He said, "I'm surprised to see you at the palace at this hour."

"But I'm a guest here. I have a beautiful little room on the third floor with a bathroom right down the hall."

"I thought you would be staying at the villa with Alice and Noah."

"Well, the truth is I asked Alice if she could get me in as a guest here at the palace instead—for the life experience, you know?" Something evasive in her expression tipped him off that "life experience" wasn't all of it.

"And because of Noah?"

She shrugged. "He's promised to stop hovering over me and to let me lead my own life, but he still thinks he knows what's best for me. Here at the palace, I'm on my own. I take care of myself without my big brother keeping tabs on where I go and when I come in at night." She loosed a gusty sigh. "Honestly, Dami. Sometimes he acts like I'm twelve instead of twenty-three."

"He loves you and wants to be certain you're safe and well."

For that she shot him an I-don't-want-to-hear-it look. He let the subject drop.

The coffee didn't take long. He poured her a cup, got out the cream and sugar and even found a couple of pastries in the bread box. He put the pastries on a serving plate, set them each a place, along with napkin, fork and spoon, and then took his own cup and settled into the chair opposite her. "There. Drink your coffee."

Obediently, she spooned in a little sugar, poured in a drizzle of cream, stirred and sipped. "It's good."

"Life is too short for bad coffee."

A sudden smile tugged at the corners of her mouth. He shook his head. "Something amuses you?"

"It's too weird, that's all. Being served coffee and sweet rolls by a prince…."

He waved a hand. "Under everyday circumstances, my man, Edgar, would prepare the coffee. But Edgar is elsewhere this morning."

She blushed again, the color flowing upward over her sweet, velvety cheeks. "Thank you, Dami. You're always so kind to me." All at once her big eyes brimmed with moisture.

"Luce?" He jumped up, went around to her and knelt by her chair, taking care as he did it that the damn robe didn't gape and embarrass them both. "What is this? Tears?"

She sniffled. "Oh, Dami…" Her scent drifted to him: cherries and soap. So very Luce. It made him want to smile.

But he didn't. He kept a solemn face as he took the silk handkerchief from the breast pocket of his robe. "Here, now. Dry your eyes."

With a sad little sigh, she dabbed at her cheeks. "I'm being ridiculous."

"You are not, nor have you ever been, ridiculous." He rose—and then hesitated, not wanting to leave her side if she was going to keep crying.

She waved his handkerchief at him. "Go on. Sit back down. Your coffee will get cold."

So he returned to his chair and took his seat. "Eat a pastry, why don't you? Your choice, raspberry or almond."

Obediently, she transferred the raspberry brioche to her plate and took a bite. The red filling clung to her lower lip and he watched as the tip of her pink tongue emerged to lick it clean. "Yum."

He prompted, "Now. What is this 'issue' that you've come to me about?"

She sucked in a long breath. "First of all…"

"Yes?"

"Oh, Dami. First I really, really need to thank you."

"But why?"

"Oh, please. You know why. For coming to my rescue when I was running out of options and had no idea what I was going to do."

He gave her a one-shouldered shrug. "You've already thanked me. Repeatedly."

"But I can never thank you enough. You came and you helped me with Noah when I couldn't get through to him and I didn't see how I ever would." Her brother had been reluctant to let her go away to fashion school in Manhattan. "I live in New York City now because of you. I live in the greatest old building with the nicest neighbors because of you." She laid her hand against her upper chest, where the tip of a pale scar was just visible above the neckline of her striped top, which she wore with great panache, along with a short, tight, floral-print skirt, a wide black belt and ankle boots. "Thank you."

"You are completely welcome. I'm glad I could help—and you were the driving force in your own liberation. You have to know that. *You* made it happen."

"But I couldn't have done it without you being willing to fly to California to save me." Her brother, Noah, owned a large estate in Carpinteria, near Santa Barbara. "You stood up for me with Noah, and you took me away." She plunked a scrap of paper on the table and pushed it toward him. "This should pay you back, at least a little."

He saw that it was a check for a large sum of money and shook his head. "Don't be absurd. Noah paid for it all." Her brother had finally seen the light and given her his blessing to follow her dream—along with the all-important backing of his enormous bank account.

"Dami, you flew me to the East Coast in your own private jet. You leased me my beautiful apartment in your amazing building without asking for a deposit or anything. And I may be way naive, but even I know that my rent is impossibly low."

"Put your money away."

She drew herself up. "No. I will not. I have my trust fund now and I'm doing fine. I owe you this money, at least." She'd grown quite stern suddenly.

And he realized that to continue refusing her in this would only be ungracious. "Fair enough. Consider me repaid in full."

A glowing smile bloomed. "Excellent."

He transferred the almond brioche to his plate and cast a second dismissive glance at her check. "So, then, was that it—the 'issue' that's been troubling you?" How disappointing, to think her blushes and nervous chatter and unwilling tears came down to a nonexistent debt she felt driven to repay.

But then she pressed her soft lips together and shook her head.

Anticipation rose in him again. "So there's more?"

She nodded. And then dipped her head and spoke to her half-eaten brioche. "You and your girlfriend, Vesuvia…?"

V? She wanted to talk about V? Whatever for? *He* certainly didn't. But she'd stalled out again. And she was still staring at her plate as though she didn't have a clue how to go on. Warily, he prompted, "What about Vesuvia?"

Her brown head shot up and she met his eyes. A tiny gasp escaped her. "I mean, she's so impossibly beautiful and glamorous and…it seems like she's always on the cover of my favorite magazines…*Vogue* and *Bazaar* and *Glamour* and *Elle*."

He arched a brow at her and asked in a tone he took care to make lighthearted, "Do you want me to introduce you to V for some reason?" God. He hoped not. But perhaps she had some idea that V might be willing to wear her designs.

"Introduce me to her? Oh, no. I don't. Not at all."

Relief had him settling more comfortably into his chair. "So, then?"

"Well, are you, um, still together with her?" The question came out in a breathy rush.

He was tempted to remind her that his relationship with V was really none of her business. But he couldn't quite bring himself to do that. He liked Lucy too much and she was far too flustered already. So he said, "No, we're not seeing each other any longer. I'm afraid it didn't work out."

Lucy stared at him rather piercingly now and he had the oddest sensation of being under interrogation. "So you're broken up, you and Vesuvia? And you're not in a relationship with anyone else?"

He couldn't help chuckling. "Yes, we are, and no, I'm not—and, Luce, my darling, don't you think it's time you told me about this so-urgent issue of yours?"

She sagged back in the chair with a groan. "Oh, Dami. It's just… Well, there's a man. A special man I met."

"A man?" He was totally lost now. From V to a *special* man?

"Yes. He's just way hot. He's an actor. He lives in my building in NoHo— Well, I mean *your* building. Brandon? Brandon Delaney?" She seemed to be prompting him.

He shook his head. "No idea."

She kept trying. "Blond hair, the most amazing butterscotch eyes…"

Dami had a property manager and a superintendent for the building and only a vague idea of who lived there. Some of the apartments were co-op, others leased. And *butterscotch* eyes? Was this a man or a dessert? "I'm afraid I don't recall this Brandon."

"Oh, Dami. He thinks I'm a *child,* you know? And I'm not a child— Well, yes, okay, I *am* inexperienced, not to mention naive. I get that. But I'm not stupid. I've simply been sick for most of my life and kind of out of the mainstream of things. But not anymore. I'm well and I'm strong and I'm living my dream. And I really, really need to get started on doing the things that normal, healthy women do—now that, at last, I *am* a normal, healthy woman. Dami, I need to, you know, hook up."

He tried not to look as befuddled as he felt. "Hook up."

"You know…have sex?"

"Er, yes. Of course I know."

"But see, I feel so awkward and strange about it." She lifted both hands and pressed them to the sides of her head, as though trying to keep what was inside from escaping. "I mean, I've met a few guys in Manhattan this past month and a half." She let go of her head and waved her slim arms about in her excitement over something of which he still had no clue. "I've met a few guys and I've tried to picture myself with one of them, but the idea of doing it with any of them just doesn't feel right—except for with Brandon. I find Brandon extremely attractive and I definitely could get something going with him. But he's very much about his acting and he's big on life experience and he won't hook up with me because he doesn't have sex with boring, innocent women."

Damien's head was truly spinning. "You…asked this Brandon fellow to…?"

"Oh, no!" More blushing. "Not straight out, I mean. I don't know him well enough to ask him straight out."

"Oh, of course. I see." He didn't, actually. Not in the least.

"But I did try to kiss him…."

"And?"

"He caught my arms and kind of held me, really gently, away from him."

"You mean you didn't kiss him after all?"

"No. He stopped it before it happened. And he looked in my eyes and told me that it could never work, that I'm so young and inexperienced and I wear my emotions on my sleeve. He said he would never want to hurt me, but of course he *would* hurt me because I would be in over my head with him. He said he doesn't, you know, sleep with virgins and that he's got no time for anything serious right now anyway, because acting is his life."

What a fatheaded ass. "You are adorable, Luce, and thoroughly charming. Don't let anyone ever tell you otherwise."

She put one of those flying hands to her heart. "Oh, Dami. See? That's how you are. Not only have you treated me like someone who matters from the first time I met you. Not only did you come to my rescue and fly me to Manhattan when I'd almost given up on ever getting there. Somehow you just instantly, always, say the exact thing that I need to hear."

He made another stab at finding out where all this was going. "So you came to me for advice, then?" He reached for his coffee cup.

And Lucy said, "No. Not advice. Sex."

He set the cup down sharply. "Say again?"

"Dami, it's so simple. I want you to have sex with me. I want you to be my first."

Chapter Two

Damien found himself experiencing the strangest sensation of complete unreality. "Dearest Luce. Did you just ask me to be your lover?"

She nodded, her shining brown head bouncing up and down as though on a spring. "Oh, yes. Please. I *like* you, Dami. I truly do. And when I think of having sex with you, it doesn't seem like it would be too awful—and you *are* so experienced. I really do need someone who can help me be more sophisticated and you just happen to be about the most sophisticated person I know. And as for having sex with you, well, you seem like you would know what you were doing and I…" The words ran out.

He started to speak but fell silent when she moaned.

And then she let out a cry and put her hands to her cheeks as though in an effort to cool her fierce blush.

"Oh, God. You should see your face. This is not going well, is it?"

"Luce, I—"

Before he could say more, she shoved back her chair and leaped to her feet. "Seriously. I don't know what I was thinking. This is a bad idea. A really stupid, utterly inane idea. And now you're going to think I'm such a complete child, a total dork…"

He got up. "No, I do not think you're a child. Truly, it's all right. It's…"

But she didn't stay to hear the rest. She whirled and bolted for the door.

"Luce!" Dami went after her and managed to catch up with her halfway down the hall to his private foyer. He grabbed her hand. "Wait."

She moaned again and tried to pull away. "Let me go."

He held on. "Please. Don't become so worked up. I promise you, you're neither a child nor a dork. And I'm quite flattered."

There was yet another moan. "Oh, no, you're not."

He lifted the hand he'd captured and kissed it lightly. Then he wrapped his other hand around their joined ones. "Listen to me."

A little whine escaped her.

"Tell me you're listening," he coaxed.

"What?" She sagged against the hallway wall, between two handsome nature prints he'd bought at one of his sister Rhia's charity art auctions. "All right. Yes, I'm listening."

"I *am* flattered." He tried a hint of a smile and watched her soft lips quiver in reluctant response. "Really, Luce, you are so unpredictable. You know, I find I never know what you might do or say next. But at the same time, at heart you are so wonderfully direct, so honest."

"Direct and honest," she grumbled, but at least she'd stopped trying to make him let go of her hand. "Ugh. So I'm a good person, but I'm not especially exciting— that's what you're saying."

"No, that is not what I'm saying."

"Yes, it is."

He moved in a fraction closer, keeping their joined hands between them, connecting them. The scent of soap and cherries was a little stronger now, sweet and tart and so very…clean. "Don't forget. I said you are unpredictable, too. That makes you exciting."

"No…."

"Yes. It does, I promise you. And may I add that you are also like a breath of fresh air, both bracing and sweet." He watched her flushed face and thought how very much he liked her, how he'd liked her from the first time he met her, at her brother's Carpinteria estate when she'd dragged him to her sewing room and showed him several of her creations, after which she'd plunked her portfolio down on the cutting table and started flipping through the pages, chattering nonstop about her ambitions as a fashion designer.

Now she gazed at him through big eyes full of hope and trust. "Oh, you do know how to dish out the compliments."

"It's easy when I'm only telling the absolute truth."

"Oh, right. Sure you are."

He turned his mouth down at the corners in a mimic of sadness. "Luce. You wound me."

She started to giggle—and then she blinked. "Wait a minute."

"Yes?"

"Are you telling me that, um, you *will?*"

Ouch. Leave it to Lucy to cut right to the heart of the matter.

The thing was, he wanted to tell her yes, that he would be her lover. He truly did. But he was no more a seducer of virgins than Brandon of the butterscotch eyes. He absolutely did find her attractive, but in the way one finds a child attractive, because she was pure and honest, innocent and sweet yet also funny and surprising and perceptive, too. Not to mention splendidly talented. However, he couldn't quite make himself think of her as a grown woman, as an eligible female he might take to his bed.

She was watching him suspiciously. "Long silence. I'm taking that for a no."

Above all, he did not want to hurt her. "You truly are lovely, Luce. Your shining seal-brown hair, those enormous eyes that tip up so playfully at the corners. That one dimple in your left cheek that's deeper than the one on the right when you smile...."

"You're an absolute genius at making me feel good-looking."

"Because you *are* good-looking."

"But you still haven't answered my question," she accused. "I'm thinking that's not a good sign."

The solution came to him. "Tell you what."

For that he got an eye roll. "Stalling. That's what you're doing, right?"

"Well, yes. I suppose that I am."

"Oh, I knew it." She wrinkled her cute nose at him. But at least she no longer seemed on the verge of shedding more tears.

He qualified, "However, I am stalling in a good way."

"Ha." She made another attempt to free her hand from his hold.

He didn't let go. "Listen. Please."

"Fine, fine." She tipped her head from side to side, her words a singsong. "Go ahead."

"We'll take things a bit slower."

That brought a frown to crease her smooth brow. "Slower than what?"

"You're here for the holiday weekend."

"I am, yes."

"We'll spend the time—or much of it, anyway—in each other's company."

"You mean like we're dating?"

"Yes. As though we were dating."

"Oh, Dami. I may be naive, but I'm so on to you. I know what you're doing. You're trying to let me down easy."

She had it right, but he had no intention of admitting that. "Come to the kitchen." He tugged on her hand again. "We can finish our coffee…." He expected her to require more coaxing and encouragements before she'd agree to sit at the table again and discuss the situation frankly.

But as she so often did, she surprised him. She said, "Yes. All right." And she followed him back the way they had come.

In the kitchen, Lucy reclaimed her seat at the table and Dami refreshed their coffee cups before settling opposite her again.

Lucy watched him. He really was so nice to look at, in his sexy black robe and all, with that slice of sculpted chest on view, with his thick dark hair and his eyes that sometimes seemed the darkest brown and then, in certain lights, a green so deep it was almost black. So different from Brandon, who was clean-cut and outdoorsy with a handsome, open sort of face. Dami exuded power and ease, a hint of danger and strangely, humor and tenderness, too. They called him the Player Prince. Everyone said he'd been with more women than her big brother, Noah. Which was seriously saying something.

Noah used to be quite the lady-killer. But in the past year or so, he'd changed. He'd stopped seeing women at all for a while. And then he'd found Dami's sister Alice. Lucy did adore Alice. Alice was perfect for Noah. Lucy felt real satisfaction knowing that she could strike out on her own and her big brother had someone to love him the way he'd never let himself be loved before. Someone to keep him honest and stand up to him when he got too full of himself.

"Luce." Dami was frowning at her. "What *are* you thinking?"

She sipped her coffee. "That my brother's happy with your sister, and I'm really glad about that." Well, she *had* been thinking about Noah and Alice—*after* she'd admired the man across from her in his sexy robe.

"They *are* good together," he agreed.

She laughed, feeling lighthearted suddenly. Okay, she got the message that Dami wasn't up for teaching her the ways of love and sex. But at least he hadn't acted as if he couldn't wait to get rid of her, the way Brandon had when she'd tried to put a move on him. Dami would still be her friend always—somehow she just knew that—no matter what gauche, immature thing she did or said.

"What is so humorous?" he demanded.

"I don't know. I was really scared to ask you. And

now I've done it, and…it's okay. The sky didn't fall. You didn't toss me out the door on my butt."

"I would never toss you out the door—on your butt or otherwise."

"Exactly. I love that about you."

He ate a little more of his pastry and then he said thoughtfully, "I do realize I have something of a reputation with women. But even someone like me doesn't instantly fall into bed with any female who wanders by, no matter how fetching and well dressed she might be." A wry smile twisted his mouth. "Or at least, I haven't for the past few years."

This was getting interesting. "You're saying you had a lot of indiscriminate sex when you were younger?"

"I suppose I did, yes."

"You suppose? Oh, come on, Dami. You did or you didn't."

He chuckled. "I like you, Luce."

She beamed. "It's totally mutual."

"And I think that spending time together over this long weekend is a way to find out if there could ever be more than friendship between us."

Yeah, okay. She fully got that he was only being nice to her. And his suggestion of the two of them together for the weekend, just having fun, wasn't what she'd come for.

But so what?

It would be wonderful to spend a whole weekend at his side. And maybe a little of his smoothness and elegance would rub off on her. That certainly couldn't hurt. She might not get the whole sex-for-the-first-time thing over with, but at least she could acquire a little sophistication—if that was possible in a few short days.

She sipped her coffee and he sipped his. When she

set her cup down, she said, "So, then. Sunday I'm flying back to New York. And you're saying it will be you and me, together in a dating kind of way, today, tomorrow and Saturday."

He inclined his dark head. "Starting this morning with the Prince Consort's Thanksgiving Bazaar on the rue St.-Georges."

Dami leaned close to her. "Ignore them," he whispered. "Simply pretend they're not there."

They stood side by side on the cobbled street, in front of a booth that sold handmade Christmas ornaments. By then it was nearing eleven in the morning. Lucy couldn't resist a quick glance over her shoulder.

The street was packed with milling holiday shoppers and the air smelled of savory meats, fried potatoes and baked goods from the numerous food booths and carts that jostled for space with the stalls offering jewelry and handmade soaps, pottery and paintings and all kinds of bright, beautiful textiles. People chatted and laughed, bargained and shouted. And there were children everywhere, some in strollers or baby carriers, some clutching the hands of their mothers or fathers. And some running free, zipping in and out among the shoppers, cause for fond amusement and the occasional cry of, "Watch out, now," or, "Slow down a tad, young man."

Even in the holiday crowd, though, it was easy to pick out the photographers lurking nearby. Each had a camera in front of his face, the wide lens trained on the Player Prince.

Dami elbowed her lightly in the side. "I said ignore them."

"But they're everywhere."

"Yes, my darling. But they know the rules within the

principality. Here they are careful to keep their distance. Believe me, it's much better than in France or England or America, where they come at you without mercy, up close and very personal, firing questions as they click away." His voice was low and teasing and almost flirtatious. Or maybe she was just reading into it after their discussion of earlier that morning. Most likely, Dami wasn't flirting at all but only being kind to her.

And she was going to completely take advantage of his kindness and love every minute of it. "What happens if they approach you?"

"Someone from the palace guard or my brother Alex's Covert Command Unit will appear from the milling throng and escort them directly to the border."

"Just like that?"

"Yes," he assured her. "Just like that."

Dami had three brothers and five sisters. Lucy had yet to meet them all. "Alex is your twin, right?"

"Yes, he is. We're identical, though no one ever has any trouble telling us apart. Alex has always been the serious one. And you know me." He gave a supremely elegant shrug. "I make it my mission in life to take *nothing* seriously."

"What is a Covert Command Unit?"

"A small, specially chosen and trained corps of Montedoran soldiers who are always at the ready to take action in a critical situation." He said this in his usual lighthearted tone.

"Seriously?"

He nodded at a passing couple and they nodded back. And then he told her, "All the family's bodyguards are from the CCU. And my sister Rhia's husband, Marcus, is one of them—and, Luce," he said indulgently, "will you please forget about the men with the cameras? To keep slipping them sideways glances only encourages them."

She laughed and caught his arm and grinned up at him. "I can't help it. Dami, you know how I am. Home-schooled. Most of my life, I hardly ever left the house—except when I had to be rushed to the hospital. I have a lot of life to catch up on. Everything fascinates me, even pushy men with cameras."

The merchant in the booth, a large woman with a wide, lined face, held up a pair of snowflake earrings, delicate and silvery, accented with tiny rhinestones that caught the late-November sunlight and twinkled festively. "Highness. For the lady...?"

Dami nodded. "Very pretty. Yes, she'll have them." He handed over the money without even a glance at Lucy for approval.

Lucy almost protested, but the woman in the booth looked so pleased and the earrings were pretty and not that expensive. Also, it did seem good practice for becoming sophisticated to pretend to be the sort of woman who casually received trinkets from a handsome prince.

The merchant put the earrings in a small cloth pouch and passed them to Dami, who gave them to Lucy. She thanked him and they moved on to the next booth, where she spotted a bright scarf she wanted and whipped out her wallet. The vendor glanced at Dami, as though expecting Dami to buy it for her.

Lucy did speak up then. "Please. Here you go...."

The vendor scowled and kept looking at Dami, who put on an expression both grim and resigned. The merchant took her money with a disapproving shake of his head. And Dami bought a child-size leather belt studded with bits of silver.

She almost turned to him then and asked why the

merchant had wanted him to pay for her scarf and what was with the child-size belt. But then, what did it matter, really? She knew already that he was generous to a fault. And maybe the belt was for one of his nephews.

As they moved on, he bought more gifts for children, boys and girls alike. He bought toy trucks and cars and any number of little dolls and stuffed animals. He bought a tea set and three plastic water pistols, Ping-Pong paddles and balls, packets of crayons, colored pencils and a stack of coloring books.

She finally asked him, "Who are all these toys for?"

He only smiled and advised mysteriously, "Wait. You'll see."

She might have quizzed him some more, but she was having far too much fun finding treasures of her own. Just about every booth seemed to have at least one small perfect thing she wanted. The bazaar was giving her so many ideas for new designs featuring the colors and textures all around her. A kind of glee suffused her. It was like a dream, *her* dream, from all those lonely shut-in years of growing up. That she would someday be well and strong and travel to exciting places and be inspired to make beautiful things that women all over the world would reach out and touch, saying, *Yes. This. This is what I want to wear.*

But wouldn't you know that Dami got quicker at detecting her choices? And the merchants all seemed to expect Dami to pay. They ignored the bills in her hand and grabbed for the ones in his.

She finally had to lean in close to him and whisper, "Okay. Enough. I mean it, Dami. If I want something, I am perfectly capable of buying it myself."

They stood, each weighed down with bags and packages, beside a flower stall where glorious bouquets of every imaginable sort of bloom stood in rows of cone-shaped containers. He bought a big bouquet of bright flowers, then took her arm and guided her to the side, out of the way of the pressing crowd. "Do you realize that this bazaar was established over thirty years ago in honor of my father, in the year that my oldest brother, Max, was born?"

"How nice. And what does that have to do with why you keep buying things for me when I have plenty of money of my own?"

"It has everything to do with it."

"I don't see how."

"My dearest Luce," he said with equal parts affection and reproach, "Thanksgiving is, after all, an American holiday. Yet Montedorans embrace it and celebrate it. They do this for my father's sake. And this bazaar was named for him because he gave my mother happiness—and a son, very quickly."

"How virile of him. And why do you sound like you're lecturing me?"

He actually shook a finger at her, though his eyes glittered playfully as he did it. "My darling, I *am* lecturing you. We celebrate Thanksgiving in Montedoro for the sake of my father, and this bazaar exists in respect for my father. And when a Bravo-Calabretti prince attends the bazaar, he tries to buy from each and every vendor, in *thanksgiving* for the gift the Montedoran people have bestowed on us, to trust us with the stewardship of this glorious land."

"Well, all right. Wonderful. You bought a bunch of things. And you paid for them. In thanksgiving. But no way are you expected to pay for *my* things."

"Don't you see? Each item I buy blesses the vendor. The *more* I buy, the better."

She laughed. "Good one. I'm actually helping you out when I let you buy my stuff."

Along with the usual all-around hotness, he was looking very pleased with himself. "That's right. And the vendor, as well. Surely you cannot deny us these blessings."

She stared at him. He looked at her so levelly under those straight dark brows. His mouth held a solemn curve. But the usual mischief danced in his eyes. She accused, "You're making this up."

"Why ever would I?" Lightly. Teasingly.

She still wasn't sure she believed him. But he had a point, she supposed. Why would he make up a story like that? And the vendors really had seemed to want him specifically to be the one to pay.

She tried to explain, "It's just that you always look like you're teasing me, Dami. Even when you're serious."

"Because I *am* teasing you—even when I'm serious."

She shifted the mountain of bags in her arms in order not to drop any. "You're confusing me. You know that, right?"

He bent a fraction closer and she caught a hint of his aftershave, which she'd always really liked. It was citrusy, spicy and earthy, too. It made her think of an enchanted forest. And true manliness. And a long black limousine. "Try to enjoy it," he said.

"Being confused?"

"Everything. Life. All these people out for the holiday. Sunshine. This moment that will never come again." Suddenly, she wanted to hug him close. There was something so…magical about him. As though he knew really good secrets and just might be willing to share them with her. He added, "And won't you please believe me? The Thanksgiving Bazaar is in my father's honor and the more I personally buy here, the happier the merchants will be."

She groaned, but in a good-natured way. "I think I give up. Buy me whatever you want to buy me."

He inclined his dark head in a so-gracious manner that made her feel as if she'd just done him a whopping favor. "Thank you, Luce. I shall."

By then they'd strolled the length of one side of the rue St.-Georges and bought goods from about half of the booths. Dami set down the bouquet of flowers and a few bags of toys and got out his phone. He made a quick call. A few minutes later two men appeared dressed in the livery of the palace guard.

The guards carried their packages for them, falling back to follow behind as they worked their way up the other side of the street, buying at least one item from each of the vendors. The ever-present photographers followed, too, snapping away, their cameras constantly pressed to their faces, but they did keep enough distance that it wasn't all that difficult to pretend they weren't there.

Midway back up the other side of the street, they came to the food-cart area, a separate little courtyard of its own in the middle of the bazaar. The carts reminded Lucy of old-fashioned circus cars, each brightly painted in primary colors, some decorated with slogans and prices and pictures of the food they served, others plastered with stenciled-on images of everything from the Eiffel Tower to jungle cats. Dami bought food from each cart—pastries, meat pies, sausages on sticks, cones of crispy fried potatoes, flavored ices, tall cups of hot chocolate. There was no way the two of them could have made a dent in all that food. But conveniently, groups of

Montedoran children had gathered around. They were only too willing to help. Dami bought food and drinks for all, while the food sellers smiled and nodded and accepted his money. Were they grateful to be so richly "blessed"? Or just pleased to be doing a brisk business?

Lucy decided it didn't matter which. Dami had been right. She was enjoying the experience, reveling in this moment that would never come again.

When they left the food carts, the children followed, falling in behind the palace guards with their high piles of packages.

Dami spotted someone he knew across the street. He waved and called out, "Max!"

The tall, gorgeous man with the unruly hair and mesmerizing glance bore a definite resemblance to the prince at her side. He returned Dami's greeting and then went back to his negotiations with a vendor who sold scented soaps and bath salts.

Lucy asked, "Your oldest brother, right?" Dami nodded. "Will he make the rounds of every booth?"

"And buy something from each one."

"No wonder the vendors feel blessed. I mean, there are nine of you, brothers and sisters together. That's a lot of blessings."

"We don't all attend every year. But we do our best to make a showing—and come on now. We still have several booths to go."

They visited the remainder of the booths, piling more packages into the arms of the two guards. When they'd finally made a stop with every vendor in the bazaar, it was nearing two in the afternoon. Neither of them was hungry, as they'd done a lot of sampling when they'd fed the children at the food carts. Thanksgiving dinner at the palace took place in the early evening, so they didn't have to hurry back to get ready.

"What next?" Lucy asked.

Dami sent one of the guards off with Lucy's purchases and orders to have them delivered to her room. "This way," he said, and took Lucy's hand.

It felt lovely, she thought, almost as though they really were together in a romantic way, her hand in his strong, warm one, the guard with all the bags of toys behind them, and a trail of laughing kids strung out along the street, following in their wake. It wasn't far down to the harbor, and that was where Dami led them, to a little square of park along the famous Promenade, which rimmed the pier where all the fabulous yachts were docked.

"Right here," he said at last, indicating an iron bench beneath a rubber tree. They sat down together and the guard put all the packages at their feet as the children found seats on the grass around them.

And then Dami began passing out the toys and coloring books, the dolls and stuffed animals, with the guard helping out to make sure everyone got something. A ring of adults stood back out of the way, and Lucy realized they were the parents of the children. Some parents had little ones in their arms or in strollers. The guard made sure even the smallest ones received a toy.

It was all so charming and orderly, like some fantasy of sharing, the children laughing and chattering together, but in such a well-behaved way. Once or twice she heard raised voices when one child wanted what another one had. But all Dami had to do was glance in that direction and the argument would cease.

When all the bags were empty and every child had

a gift, Dami asked the gathered children, "Would you like to hear a story?"

A happy chorus of yeses went up.

And Dami launched into a story about a little boy and a magic book, a laughing dragon and a secret passage into a special kingdom where a kind princess ruled with a gentle hand. There was an evil giant who never bothered to bathe or brush his teeth. The giant captured the princess. And the little boy and the laughing dragon rescued her with the help of spells from the magic book.

When the story was over, the children and the ring of adults applauded and the children cried, "One more, Prince Dami! Only one more!"

He obliged them with a second story, this one about a brave girl who saved Montedoro from an evil wizard who'd cast a sleeping spell across the land. Applause followed that story, too, and a few called, "One more!"

But Dami only laughed and shook his head and wished them all a richly blessed Thanksgiving. The children went to find their parents and Dami took her hand again and pulled her to her feet.

"That was wonderful," she told him. "Did you make up those stories yourself?"

A so-Gallic shrug. "I'm not that clever. They are Montedoran folk tales, two of many. A century and a half ago a Montedoran named Giles deRay gathered them into a couple of volumes, *Folk Tales of Montedoro.* We all know the stories. It's something of a tradition over the holidays for the princes of Montedoro to pass out gifts they've bought at the bazaar and tell the children a few of the old tales."

"What a beautiful tradition."

He was watching her, a half smile curving those killer lips of his. "You find everything beautiful. I think, Luce, that you are the happiest person I have ever known."

His words warmed her. "I prefer happiness. It's so much more fun than the alternative."

"You sound like Lili, my brother Alex's wife— Liliana, Crown Princess of Alagonia."

"Oh, yes. I've heard of her. And Alagonia is an island country off the coast of Spain, correct?"

"Yes. We—my brothers and sisters and I—grew up with Lili. My mother and Lili's mother, Queen Evelyn, were great friends. Lili was always the nicest person in the room. Of course, she ended up with Alex, who was not nice at all. The good news is that he's much better now since he's made a life with Lili."

"Are they happy, your brother and Princess Lili?"

"They are, yes. Ecstatically so."

"I'm glad. And you've got me thinking. Can a person be both happy *and* sophisticated?"

He did the loveliest thing right then. He touched her, just the lightest caress of a touch as he traced his finger down her jaw to her chin and tipped her face up fully to him. "What? You're afraid you'll have to choose?"

Her tummy felt all fluttery and her pulse beat faster. Oh, he was very, very good at pretending they were dating. "I don't want to choose—but if I had to, I would choose happiness."

He moved a fraction closer, his finger still touching her chin. "It's good to know you have your priorities in order."

"Dami?"

"Yes?"

"Are you going to kiss me?" Somehow she had let her eyes drift to half-mast.

"Would you like that?" he whispered, his smooth, low voice playing a lovely tune all along her nerve endings.

She couldn't stifle the soft, eager sound that came from her throat. "Oh, that would be fabulous. Yes."

"Are you sure? The paparazzi are watching. A kiss would definitely make the tabloids."

She couldn't hold back a giggle. "Oh, come on." She opened her eyes a little and saw that he was smiling down at her, a tender sort of smile that made her tummy more fluttery than ever. "It's too late to back out now."

"Luce, you are so innocent—and yet so delightfully bold."

"Bold. Good. I like that a lot. As a matter of fact, I…"

There was more she'd meant to say. But at that moment, the ability to form words deserted her.

His warm, soft, wonderful mouth settled, gentle as a breath, on hers.

Chapter Three

Kissing Luce.

And not on the cheek. Not a swift brush across the mouth in passing. Not on the forehead or the tip of her cute nose.

Kissing Luce in the *real* way.

Damien hadn't actually planned to do that.

But her sweet pink lips were tipped up to him and her bright brown eyes were halfway shut and she managed to look so very inviting in her adorable clean-scrubbed, cheerfully angelic sort of way.

Plus there had been the joy of the day with her—and really, there was no other word for it. Joy. Lucy Cordell was a joy. The world through her eyes was a magical place. A good and generous place, a place of endless wonder and simple, perfect pleasures. To see the world with her, through her eyes, was a fine and satisfying experience indeed.

But he'd already known that. Every time he saw her, it was like that. The world was fresh and new again and he would do anything to hear her laugh, to watch her smile.

However, the kiss?

No. The kiss had not been in his clever plan to enjoy the weekend with her, to offer her his company and a large helping of Montedoran tradition and then send her back to New York as innocent as ever.

Kisses, *real* kisses, didn't fit in the plan.

But in the end, how could he resist?

His mouth touched hers and she let out the tiniest, most tender of sighs. Her sweetness flowed into him.

And it was...

More.

Much more than he had expected. Far beyond the boundaries of what he'd intended.

It was a light kiss, a gentle kiss. His mouth against hers, but chastely. Not in any way a soul kiss.

And yet, still, a revelation.

He breathed in the scent of cherries and he saw, all at once, what he had been able to keep from himself before. He saw that she was sweet and innocent, yes.

But she was not a child.

And now that he'd done it, now that he'd felt her lips against his, breathed in her breath, listened to her tiny sigh, he wasn't going to be able to unring that bell. The spilled milk would not flow back into the bottle. The cat was out and was prowling around now, thoroughly unwilling to go back in the bag.

Henceforth and forever, when he looked at Lucy, he would see a grown woman. A grown woman he could so easily desire.

The temptation tugged at him to reach out and gather

her closer, to deepen the kiss, to explore this new Lucy, the one he hadn't let himself see before. And why not? He'd never been a man who put much store in resisting temptation. What was the point? Better to give in. Life was too short and pleasure too...pleasurable.

But somehow and for some reason he didn't even understand, he kept his hands to himself. He lifted his head and she opened her eyes and he felt absurdly, ridiculously proud of himself.

"Oh, Dami," she whispered happily, searching his face.

He touched her neat little chin again, because he could. Her skin was poreless, creamy, fresh. "It was only a kiss," he shamelessly lied.

She corrected him with a glowing smile, "An absolutely perfect kiss."

He offered his arm. She took it. Together they turned for the car that waited to take them back to the palace.

Thanksgiving dinner at the Prince's Palace was a family affair. A very large family affair. Large enough to be held in the ornate formal dining room of the State Apartments. It was to be dressy but not formal.

Lucy wore a plum-colored lace creation of her own with little satin straps over the shoulders and a skirt that came to just above her knees. Her deep purple satin pumps had big satin bows at the heels. The dress showed enough skin that she didn't look *too* innocent, but the cut was more youthful than clingy and that made it nice for a family affair.

At first they all gathered in the Blue Room next to the dining room. Drinks were served. She didn't spot Dami right away, but she did see Noah and Alice on the far side of the room talking to another couple Lucy didn't recognize. Alice wore a gorgeous copper-colored dress and held Noah's arm and he smiled down at her with such a look of love and contentment Lucy found herself grinning in satisfaction at the sight.

But then she got worried that Noah might see her and wave at her to join them. She did love her big brother, but the last thing she needed was him hovering over her. He could be like some fussy old mother hen with her.

Objectively, she couldn't blame him for wanting to look after her. They'd lost both their parents way too soon and he had a deep-rooted fear that something awful would happen to her. She'd been ill so much growing up that his fear only intensified. Any number of times, Noah had found just the right specialist to save her at the last minute when she was at death's door. She loved him, she did. He was the best big brother in the world. And he kept promising he understood that she was ready to run her own life now. Sometimes she believed him. And sometimes she wondered if he was ever going to get off her case.

She circled away to another side of the room, putting a large gold-veined Ionic column between her and Noah. Perfect. Now she was completely out of his line of sight.

"Your dress is adorable and your shoes are very naughty." The deep, smooth voice came from directly behind her.

She turned. "Dami. There you are." He wore a beautiful dark suit and he was hands down the best-looking man in the room, which was really saying something, since all the Bravo-Calabretti princes were totally sighworthy, including Dami's father, Evan, the prince consort.

He handed her a crystal flute. "Champagne?"

She took it. They raised their glasses and she took a fizzy sip. "Yum."

"Happy Thanksgiving."

She watched his mouth move and a little shiver slid through her. Her lips kind of tingled. It might have been a few leftover bubbles from the champagne—or it might have been that she couldn't help remembering the kiss that afternoon.

How could a simple soft press of his mouth to hers be so very exciting? She might not be all that experienced, but everyone knew that an intimate, sexy kiss was wet and usually involved tongues. The kiss by the Promenade had been nothing like that.

And yet, somehow, *everything* like that.

She had to keep reminding herself not to get her hopes up, that Damien's kindness and generosity to her during this special weekend meant he cherished her friendship —and nothing more.

"Come." He took her bare arm, causing havoc beneath her skin, a sensation equally exquisite and disorienting. "I must introduce you to my parents, who will soon be your brother's in-laws."

She ordered her feet in their high satin heels to go where he took her.

Her Sovereign Highness Adrienne of Montedoro and her prince consort, Evan, were every bit as gracious and friendly as Dami and Alice. Adrienne, who had to be at least in her mid-fifties but looked forty at the most, said she'd heard so much about Noah's sister and was pleased to get to meet her at last. She knew of Lucy's ambition to work in fashion and she complimented Lucy's dress and got her to confess that, yes, it was her own design. Evan asked about when her first semester at the Fashion Institute of New York would begin.

"Right after New Year's," she said. Her feet hardly seemed to touch the inlaid marble floor as Dami led her into the dining room. "They're amazing, your parents."

"I'm afraid I have to agree with you."

"I can't believe they knew so much about me—let alone remembered what they'd heard."

"Luce. They're not young, but they're hardly to the age where the memory starts to fail."

"Oh, stop. You know what I mean. Your mother rules this country and has nine children and their spouses and *their* children to keep up with. And yet she still manages to recall that her future son-in-law's little sister, whom she's never met, wants to be a fashion designer."

"Yes, she's a marvel," he agreed matter-of-factly. "Everyone says so—and here we are." He pulled back a gilded chair with a blue damask seat.

She sat down and he took the chair beside her. There were place cards, creamy white, lettered in flowing black script. "It's so nice that we somehow ended up seated together."

He took the chair beside her and leaned close. "I'm on excellent terms with the staff."

She faked a disapproving glance. "You got someone to mess with the seating chart."

"I requested a slight rearrangement."

With a laugh, she leaned closer. "And I'm so glad you did."

The woman seated on his other side spoke to him and he turned to answer her. Lucy took that moment to soak up the wonders around her. The dining room was as beautiful as the Blue Room. The walls here were scrolled and sculpted in plaster, blue and white, with more of those gold-veined Ionic pillars marching down one wall, interspersed with mirrors. The floor was gold-

and-white inlaid marble in star and sun patterns, the coffered ceiling a wonder in gold and brown, turquoise and cream. Giant turquoise, gold and crystal Empire-style chandeliers cast a magical light over everything.

The long dining table with its endless snowy cloth, gold candlesticks and gold-rimmed monogrammed china seated thirty. Every seat was occupied.

Including the one five seats down across the table, where her brother, Noah, sat next to Alice.

Of course, Noah was looking right at Lucy. And frowning. When he saw that she'd noticed him, he slid a glance at Dami and then back to her, making it all too clear he didn't like her choice of a dinner companion.

Which was totally crappy and hypocritical of him. After all, he and Dami had been friends first, bonding a little more than two years ago now over their mutual interest in spectacular cars and fabulous women. Noah seemed to have some idea that Dami wasn't really her friend, that Dami was only out to make her another notch on his bedpost.

Which just made her want to laugh. Because hadn't she tried to convince Dami to do just what Noah was so afraid he would do? And hadn't Dami been a complete sweetheart about it, letting her down so easy she was still floating several inches above the inlaid floor?

The older gentleman on Lucy's other side spoke to her. "What a positively charming frock."

She put Noah firmly from her mind and turned to the old guy with a friendly smile and a soft, "Thank you."

He had thick white hair, wore a smoking jacket and sported a Colonel Sanders goatee. "Count Dietrich Von-Delft," he said. "Her Highness Adrienne is my second cousin once removed."

She gave the old fellow her name, explained her relationship to the Bravo-Calabretti family and told him how much she was enjoying her holiday weekend in Montedoro. He said she was very lovely, a breath of fresh air—at which point she started suspecting he might be putting a move on her.

On her other side, Dami chuckled. That gave her an excuse to turn to him. The gleam in his eyes told her he knew exactly what the count had been up to. She chatted with Dami about nothing in particular for a few minutes. And then the first course was served.

Through the meal, she tried not to look at her brother and not to get too involved in any conversations with "Richie," as the count insisted she call him. He actually was kind of sweet, but he leaned too close and he looked at her as though he wouldn't mind helping her out of her so-charming "frock." It was kind of flattering, if also a bit creepy. She did want to learn about lovemaking, but not from a guy old enough to be her grandfather.

After the meal, they all returned to the Blue Room, where after-dinner drinks were served and Prince Evan gave a nice speech about how wonderful it was to have his family around him on Thanksgiving night. There was music, a pianist and a singer who performed Broadway standards and holiday tunes, but not very loud, so everyone could visit. Lucy met more Bravo-Calabrettis. She managed to steer clear of her big brother, which was great. But then there was Count Richie. He seemed to constantly pop up out of nowhere, grinning flirtatiously through his goatee, every time she turned around. She treated him politely every time and then slipped away at the first opportunity.

Around eleven-thirty the party began to break up. Princess Adrienne reminded them that the annual Thanksgiving Candlelight Mass would be held at midnight in the St. Catherine of Sienna Chapel in the palace courtyard.

Dami took her hand and wrapped it around his arm and they followed along with the others, outside and down the wide stone stairs to the chapel. It was a beautiful service, though Lucy hardly understood a word of it. She enjoyed the flowing beauty of the priests' robes, the spicy smell of the incense, the glow of all the candles and the beautiful voices of the men and women in the choir.

When it was over, Dami led her back to the Blue Room, where more refreshments were served. They lingered for a while, visiting with his two youngest sisters, Genevra and Rory.

Finally, at about one-thirty, he walked her upstairs.

Damien stood with Lucy at the door to her room.

The hallway, narrower than the one outside his apartment, was lit by wall sconces turned down to a soft glow.

"I don't want you to go," Lucy said in that enchanting way she had of simply saying whatever popped into her mind.

He felt the same, reluctant to leave her, and that struck him as odd. He would see her in the morning after all. She still had her hand wrapped snugly around his arm. She let go—but then she caught his fingers. Her touch was cool and somehow wonderful. "Come in. Please. Just for a moment."

He knew what waited on the other side of the door. A single room with a bed, a chair or two, an armoire and maybe a small desk. It seemed inappropriate for him to go in there with her, and he found his reluctance absurd. Just because there was a bed didn't mean they had to use it.

He said, though he did know that he shouldn't, "Just for a minute or two—why not?"

"Yes!" She pulled him in.

It was just as he'd pictured it. Her bags and packages from the Thanksgiving Bazaar were piled atop the armoire. The maid had been in and turned down the bed.

She stood on the rug in the center of the room, her hands behind her, looking very young. "I should have something to offer you...."

He gave her a sideways look and a half smile. "How about a chair?"

Both hands appeared from behind her and waved around a bit. "Take your choice." He chose the one under the small window. She sat in the other, crossed her slim legs and smoothed her lacy skirt. "I had an amazing time tonight."

"You always have an amazing time."

She tipped her head from side to side as though reciting some rhyming verse in her head. "You're right. I do. I can't help it. Especially now, here in Montedoro, where I feel like I'm living in my own private fairy tale."

"Complete with a lecherous old aristocrat in an ancient smoking jacket."

She laughed, a happy little sound. He thought of V for some reason. Of the differences between Luce and V. V would have been brassed off to have some old man following her around trying to flirt with her. Not Lucy. Lucy had been patient with Richie. Patient and kind. "He was actually very sweet. But a little bit... relentless."

"A *little* bit?"

"Okay, a lot. But I liked him, though, and I didn't want to hurt his feelings."

"I know you didn't." His own voice surprised him. Too low. Too...intimate.

She almost smiled, her soft lips pursing just the slightest bit, so the dimple in her left cheek started to happen but then didn't quite. He stared at the white flesh of her throat and wondered what it would feel like to kiss her there, to scrape that softness lightly with his teeth.

And that was when he knew he needed to get out. Now. He stood.

A tender little "Oh!" escaped her and she jumped up, as well. "You're going already?"

"I really should." Something was the matter with him. He seemed unable to master his own voice. First too low, now too stiff.

"But I..." She hesitated.

"What?" Now he sounded ridiculously hopeful. What was this? He hardly knew himself—his voice not his own, his heart pounding away in the cage of his chest as though hoping somehow to break free. You'd think he was twelve again, surviving his first crush.

She settled back onto the heels of those naughty satin shoes. "You're right. I have to let you go." Regretful. Resigned. And then she smiled, her gamine face lighting up from within. "I mean, you've been amazing and there's always tomorrow."

His shoes were moving, carrying him with them. Suddenly he was standing an inch away from her. She gazed up at him and he saw there were gold and green striations caught in the velvet brown of her eyes. "Yes," he heard himself say, "tomorrow..."

And then he was doing what he had no intention of doing, lifting a hand, brushing a finger down the side of that white throat, bending close to her, capturing that soft, slightly parted mouth.

So good. Her breath tasted of apples, fresh. Sweet. He touched her lower lip with his tongue, testing the warmth and the wonderful softness.

She let out a throaty little sound.

And then she lifted her slim arms and wrapped them around his neck. He followed suit, sliding his hands over the dusky, soft lace in the curve of her waist, gathering her in, deepening the kiss that was not supposed to happen.

Her body fit against him, slim and warm and soft. Her breasts pressed into his chest.

So good. Too good.

He felt what he wasn't ever going to feel with her: heat. Tightness. He was starting to grow hard.

That did it. Arousal woke him from the trance that had somehow settled over him. Slowly, gently, with great care, he clasped her slender waist again, lifted his mouth from hers and pushed back from her just enough that she wouldn't feel him growing thicker and harder against her belly.

She gazed up at him, eyes dreamy, still smiling. "Um. Good night," she whispered.

"Night, Luce." Miraculously, he had regained command of his own voice. He sounded so calm, completely relaxed, in full command of himself, though he was none of those things at that moment.

He let her go and turned for the door, and he didn't stop moving until he was on the other side of it and it was firmly shut behind him.

* * *

Alone in his apartment, Damien poured himself a last brandy.

His cell phone vibrated. He took it out of his pocket and saw it was V. He didn't answer. There was no point in talking to her. She would only yammer at him as usual, saying all the things he'd heard a thousand times before. It was an endless loop with V, a train on a circular track going round and round. He refused to get back on that train. How clear could he make it? He was off the train and staying off.

But he did check his voice mail: three messages. All from V. He deleted each one before she got out more than a few annoyed, impatient words.

And then he set the phone on a side table and drank his brandy and told himself the weekend with Lucy needed to stop. He couldn't afford to spend tomorrow and the next day with her. He would have to back out of the rest of their time together.

Somehow.

It had been a giant mistake, his clever plan to turn her down without hurting her tender feelings. It had become a trap for him, a trap of his own making. It was the problem of the bell that couldn't be unrung, the cat out of the bag, the milk spilled on the ground.

She had started it, started the change in the way he thought of her. She'd done it when she'd asked him to make love to her. She'd put that impossible idea into his head and before he knew it, he was starting to see her in a whole different light. And now he couldn't stop thinking of doing exactly what she'd asked him to do.

Now all of the things he liked best about her—the easy charm, the pleasure she took in every smallest thing, the complete lack of drama, her authenticity and straightforwardness, her kindness to old Dietrich—all those things worked as a snare for him.

She enchanted him.

Thoroughly.

He hadn't missed the cold glances Noah kept giving him during dinner—and afterward. Noah did not approve of Damien spending so much time with his sweet baby sister.

Damien got that. And now that he'd started to see Lucy as a potential lover, he didn't much approve of it, either. It wasn't a good idea. If Dami and Lucy did end up in bed together, well, what then? Would a sweet, naive girl like Luce really be ready to simply enjoy the experience and then move on?

No. He couldn't see it. And that meant that he had no right to keep on with this.

Somehow, tomorrow he had to find a way to let her know that their long weekend together was over after just one day.

Something wasn't right with Damien, Lucy kept thinking after he left her room.

He'd acted so strangely. Jumping to his feet out of nowhere, telling her he had to go—and then stepping right up close and kissing her, a beautiful, sexy, romantic kiss. And then racing off as though he couldn't get away from her fast enough.

Talk about mixed signals. Just when he started acting as if maybe he could see her in a man/woman way after all, he'd yanked open the door and left her standing there with her lips all tingly from his kiss and her yearning arms empty. Something had definitely spooked him.

And come on, wasn't it obvious what?

Noah.

Had to be. Those dark looks Noah had been sending her? No doubt he'd been sending them to Dami, too. Those looks must have gotten to Dami.

It wasn't right. And Lucy was not putting up with it. She needed to fix the problem. And the more she considered the situation, the more it seemed clear that she needed to fix it tonight.

So she changed into jeans, a slouchy sweater and her favorite Chuck Taylor high-tops, and off she went, along one corridor and then another, down a couple of flights of stairs and yet another hallway to a side entrance where a uniformed guard took her name and entered it into his handheld device. Then, with a brisk bow, he opened the door for her and out she went into the middle of the Montedoran night.

It wasn't that far of a walk to Alice's villa in the adjacent ward of Monagalla. And she was moving fast, wanting to get there and get the confrontation over with. It wasn't fun having it out with Noah. He was a great guy, but he had that little problem of being so sure he knew it all—including what was good for Lucy—even when he didn't. There could be shouting.

Too bad. She'd fought long and hard for her independence and her big brother could not take it back from her now.

She found Alice's villa easily enough. Her high-tops made no noise on the cobbled street. Lucy ran up the stone steps and stood in the glow from the iron fixture above the door, ringing the bell.

Nobody answered at first. Probably because it was after two in the morning. But she knew they were in there. Where else would they be?

Finally, after five rings, the door was drawn back. Michelle Thierry, Alice's assistant and housekeeper, stood on the other side clutching her plain blue robe at the neck, her pale hair flattened on one side, looking half asleep.

Lucy almost felt guilty. Yeah, okay. She probably should have had it out with Noah earlier—like the first time he'd shot her one of those disapproving looks. Maybe she shouldn't have spent the previous evening evading him. Two-thirty in the morning wasn't exactly the best time for a family chat.

"Miss Lucy," Michelle said, her voice brisk even though her eyelids drooped sleepily. "What a complete surprise. Is there an emergency?"

Too late to back down now. Lucy drew herself up. "Sort of—I mean, there is to me. I need to talk to my brother."

Michelle blinked away the last cobwebs of sleep and stepped back. "Well, I'll just go and wake him, why don't I?"

"Thank you. That would be excellent."

Michelle ushered her into the living area, with its fat, inviting sofas, comfortable chairs and beautiful antiques. "Do make yourself at home. I'll tell him you're here."

"We already know. Thank you, Michelle," said Alice from the doorway. She also wore a robe, a gorgeous red silk one painted with flowers and vines. Her brown hair was loose, tangled on her shoulders. Noah, in sweats, his hair looking blenderized and a scowl on his face, stood directly behind her. "Go back to bed," Alice added softly to Michelle.

With a nod, the housekeeper left them.

"What the hell, Lucy?" Noah grumbled as soon as the three of them were alone.

Alice pulled him down onto the sofa beside her and asked Lucy, "Are you hungry? Thirsty?"

Lucy perched on a chair. "No. I just need to get a few things clear with my brother, that's all. Then I'll let you both go back to bed."

Noah raked his hair with both hands and grumbled, "Is there some reason this couldn't wait until morning?"

She ignored the question and demanded, "Did we or did we not have an agreement about who runs my life?"

He shook his head and muttered something unpleasant under his breath. Alice sent him a warning look, one he pretended not to catch.

Lucy let out a hard breath. "Well, since you're not going to answer me, I'll answer for you. We *do* have an agreement. I run my life and *you* don't interfere."

"Interfere? What? I didn't—"

"Don't say you didn't, Noah. You know you did. You were giving me dirty looks all night long."

He did more grumbling under his breath. Alice took his hand and twined her fingers with his, but she didn't say anything. She didn't jump in to ease the tension, didn't take his side just to please him. That Noah's fiancée didn't rush to appease him made Lucy love her all the more. Finally, he came out with it. "What's going on with you and Damien?"

"Is that in any way your business?"

"Of course it's my business. You're my sister and I love you. And you said that you and Damien were just friends. *He's* said that the two of you are just friends. But you weren't acting like just friends tonight."

She reminded herself that she had absolutely nothing to hide. "We *are* friends and we always will be and we're spending the weekend together in a, er, dating kind of way."

"A…dating kind of way?" Noah looked at her as though she'd lost her mind and stood in grave danger of never finding it again.

She hitched her chin higher. "That's right. Dami and I are dating. For the weekend. We're…finding out if we might want to, um, take it to the next level." Okay, she had nothing to hide, but still. She wasn't quite willing to admit that she'd asked Dami to be her first lover. No matter how she phrased that, she didn't think it was the kind of thing her big brother needed to know.

"Dating," he repeated in a low, angry growl. "Dating for the weekend."

"Isn't that what I just said?"

Noah yanked his hand free of Alice's and shot to his feet. "No! Uh-uh. Absolutely not."

Lucy stood, too. No way she was letting him tower above her. "You have nothing to say about it, Noah. Nothing. At. All. And that's why I'm here tonight. To remind you that you are not in any way the boss of me and you need to get that through your thick—"

"Lucy, come on. Damien? Are you insane?"

"Wonderful. Now I'm crazy. Great, Noah. Fabulous."

He speared his fingers through his hair again—and dialed it back a notch. "All right. Sorry. I meant that you're…not thinking clearly."

"Whatever you meant, it was crappy. And you're wrong."

"I'm only trying to make you see that you need to get real here. Damien's not a guy who's ever in it for the long haul. He'll hurt you, break your heart. Why do you want to do that to yourself? Where's the win for you in that?"

"I think you're wrong about Dami, too. But that's not the point."

"Of course it's the point."

"No. The point is that it's my decision what happens between me and Dami—well, mine and Dami's. You have no say in what goes on between him and me. And I want you to admit that, to keep your word and get your nose out of my life like you promised me a month and a half ago that you would."

"But you can't—"

"Noah. Yes, I can." She took the few steps that brought her right up in his furious face and then she planted her feet wide, folded her arms across her middle and said, "Stay out of it. Leave it alone. Leave Dami alone. He doesn't deserve to have you all over his case just because he's willing to show me around Montedoro and treat me like a queen."

"She's right, Noah," said Alice, surprising them both by speaking up quietly from her seat on the sofa after staying out of it so completely until then. "You've said what you wanted to say and Lucy's heard every word. Now you need to back off and remember that she's all grown up and fully in charge of her own life and affairs."

Oh, yeah, Lucy thought. Alice was so the best thing that had ever happened to Noah—not to mention a true friend to Lucy in the bargain.

At that moment, Noah thought otherwise. He whirled on Alice and opened his mouth to light into her. She stared straight back at him, her body perfectly relaxed but fire in her eyes. And he shut his mouth without speaking, turned on his heel and went to the French doors that looked out on the night.

For several fairly awful seconds, nobody said a word.

Alice caught Lucy's eye and gave her a tiny nod, one

that seemed to say it would all work out. Lucy nodded back, hoping against hope that Alice had it right.

And then, at last, Noah turned to face the room again. "I don't like it."

Lucy straightened her shoulders. "Got that. Loud and clear. Will you stay out of it?"

He shut his eyes, winced—and then he muttered wearily, "Just…try not to get your heart broken. Please."

Her eyes felt kind of misty suddenly. "I will be fine. I promise you—and *will* you stay out of it? I need you to say it. I need your word that you'll leave it alone."

He rubbed at his jaw and looked away again, toward the night beyond the glass doors.

She asked a third time. "Noah. Will you?"

And finally, he faced her once more. He let out a low sound, raised both arms to the sides—and then dropped them hard. "Yeah. Fine. I'll stay out of it."

Like pulling teeth sometimes, getting him to say what she needed to hear. But at least he *had* said it. And she actually did believe him. "Oh, Noah…." She went to him.

He opened his arms and gathered her close. She teared up all over again when he whispered, "Damn. This should be easier…."

"I love you, big brother."

He hugged her even tighter. And then, as he'd promised to, he let her go. "Stay here tonight. It's way too late to wander around Montedoro by yourself."

She shook her head. "It's not far back to the palace and I'll go straight there. Don't worry, I'll be fine."

"But you—"

"Noah." Alice got up and went to him. She took his hands and put them at her waist and lifted her arms to link them around his neck. "Darling…"

He scowled down at her. "What?"

"Lucy will be perfectly safe."

"But I don't think—"

"Her choice. Her life. Remember?"

He muttered something Lucy couldn't quite make out. Alice laughed. And Noah bent and whispered something in her ear. She laughed again. Finally, he spoke to Lucy. "Good night," he said resignedly.

She escaped quickly before he could think of more reasons why she should stay.

At the palace, she went back in through the side door she'd used when she left. The same guard was there. He ushered her inside and then punched at his handheld device again, probably checking her off as safely returned.

By then it was after three. Past bedtime and then some. She went up to her room and flopped down on the bed and pressed her fingertips to the ridge of scar tissue between her breasts and thought about how she ought to be tired.

But she wasn't. It was a miracle, really, to be so strong. To stay up half the night, to run down the hill called Cap Royale on which the Prince's Palace stood, have a big fight with her brother and then run back up again—and still have energy to spare.

She was wide-awake. In fact, she just knew she wouldn't be able to sleep yet.

Not until she'd talked to Dami.

Yes. Absolutely. She needed to talk to Dami right away.

Tonight.

Chapter Four

Damien woke when the knocking started.

He squinted at the digital clock by the bed. Three thirty-six on Friday morning. And he knew instantly who it would be.

Lucy, of course, with some issue she just *had* to settle now.

He wasn't annoyed, though he absolutely ought to have been. And it never even occurred to him not to get up and answer. He did, however, take a moment to pull on a soft pair of trousers and a black sweater.

When he reached the outer door of his apartment, he hesitated, aware of a rising sensation in his midsection, of the too-rapid beating of his heart: anticipation.

Yes.

Excitement.

Definitely.

He smiled to himself. He was being absurd. How

could he just *know* it would be Lucy? And why was he rushing to the door when he fully intended to call an early end to their time together?

Ridiculous. Laughable.

It was probably only some random palace guest lost on the wrong floor, knocking on the nearest door in hopes of being pointed in the right direction.

The knock came again. He opened the door.

And there she was just as he'd known she would be, in a big floppy sweater and skinny little jeans and the cutest pair of pink high-top canvas shoes.

Something disconcerting happened inside his chest. He rigorously ignored it. "Luce. My darling." He lounged against the door frame and tried to look exhausted and thoroughly put out. "Did you notice? It's past three in the morning and once again you've dragged me from my comfortable bed."

She glowed at him. "It's really late, I know. I'm being unbelievably rude. I hope you'll forgive me, but I have to talk to you."

Just as he'd expected. She *had* to talk to him.

No. Absolutely not. He needed to gently but firmly send her away. And then tomorrow at a decent hour, he could take her aside and explain to her that he'd seen the light as to their holiday weekend together. He hated to back out on her, but the whole thing was off.

Yes. That was exactly what he should do.

He peeled himself off the door frame, stepped back and pulled the door wider. "Do you want coffee?"

"No, nothing. Just to talk." She chose the first door off the entry, which led to his sitting room. He gestured toward the two sofas facing each other on either side of the fireplace with its carved Louis Quinze red-marble mantel. She took one sofa and he took the other.

He felt way too excited and also on edge. So he made a show of getting comfortable, resting one arm along the sofa back, hitching one ankle across his knee. "What brings you from bed at this time of the night?"

She leaned toward him and braced her forearms on her thighs, folding her hands in front of her knees. "Oh, I haven't been to bed yet. I went to see Noah."

The back of his neck went tight. He lifted his hand from the sofa and rubbed at it. "You dragged him from bed, too?"

"I'm afraid I did, yeah."

"And how did that go?"

"It was pretty rocky." Her expression belied her words. She was grinning, pleased with herself.

"Luce. What are you telling me?"

She sighed and sagged back against the cushions. "The weekend. That's what we've got, you and me, to maybe make something happen. I've got no time to fool around here. I realized I needed to deal with Noah right away. He was giving me dirty looks all night. And I know he was looking at you the same way."

He tried a lazy shrug—though he didn't feel the least lazy. "It's hardly a surprise that he wouldn't be happy seeing the two of us together. Your brother's my friend. But he doesn't want me paying too much attention to his sister. He sees that there's no future in that for either of us and he doesn't want you hurt."

She sat forward again. "That's pretty much what he said. But we both know he was wrong. You won't do anything to hurt me. You would never hurt me, Dami. It's not how you are."

"Luce. That's exactly how I am. Don't you know about me? I grow bored too easily. And when I do, I move on."

She raised her hands, spread them wide and then waved them in circles. "Oh, don't be silly. You know what I mean. We have an understanding. You're, er, helping me, or you *might* help me. I mean, we're being together in a dating sort of way, and then maybe, if the feeling is right, we'll get down to the part where we take off our clothes and have great sex… Well, I mean, I would hope that it would be great. But even if it isn't, that's okay, too. I mean, I've heard that it's often pretty awkward the first time and I…" She let the words trail off as color flooded upward over her sweet round cheeks. "Ugh. I seriously hope to become more smooth and sophisticated by hanging with you. So far it's not happening."

He wanted to tell her she didn't need to be sophisticated. She was far too enchanting already. But extolling her charms was not the goal here. "And did you explain to Noah that you plan to end up in my bed?"

Her slim back snapped straight. "Are you kidding me? Please. Some things are none of his business—including what's really going on between you and me."

Dami reminded himself again that he needed to tell her this had to stop. But he kept forgetting what he needed to do because of what he *wanted* to do—which was to touch her. He ached to get up and sit on the other sofa with her, and the ache made a very distracting prickly feeling beneath his skin. He said flatly, "Your brother only wants you to be happy."

"Oh, Dami, come on. What he wants is for me to be *safe*. And to him that means under his control. If he had it his way, I would be back in California sitting around in my room. He wants me to be where he can check on me at regular intervals just to make certain I don't need medical attention, stat, even though I've been well and strong for two years now. He still has issues because our parents died, because of all the times I *almost* died. He's getting better at letting me make my own decisions about things, but he's not all the way there yet."

As always, she was thoroughly out-talking him—which on the one hand, he found frustrating. On the other hand, he only wanted her to go on talking. He only wanted to get up and sit on the other sofa with her and hear her lovely, breathless voice in his ear as he brushed his hand against her cheek and breathed in the scent of her skin and pressed his lips to her hair.

He stayed where he was and soldiered on. "I'm trying to tell you that Noah's right to be annoyed with you and to be angry at me."

"No. No, he is not right. He's out of line. Which is why I went to the villa and woke him up and told him so."

"Luce, I—"

She barreled right over him. "And I know that it bothered you, him giving you those angry looks. He's your friend and he's been acting like such a jerk to you. That wasn't right. But it's okay now. Really. You don't have to worry about it anymore. It took some doing—and Alice's help—but I finally got through to Noah."

"Tonight? You're saying you worked it all out with him tonight?" It was the last thing he'd expected.

She nodded eagerly. "I did, yes. Tonight. He's promised to stop with the deadly glances. And to totally get off my case. Honestly, he won't be embarrassing either of us with any big-brother scenes, I can promise you that."

Did he believe her? "You're certain about this?"

"Yes. Of course I'm certain. We argued. Alice backed me. And at the end, I asked Noah to stay out of it and he promised that he would. Then he hugged me and he let me go. It was another big step for him. Really. Like I said, he's getting better." She was waving her arms about as usual, hands swooping and diving like soaring doves. "He's learning to accept that I'm an adult with my own life, a life that is completely independent from him."

Dami realized he did believe her. If there was any doubt that Noah had surrendered this particular field, he would have been able to see it in her adorable open face by now.

Not that it really mattered whether Noah was leaving it alone or not. Noah had never been the problem, not really. Dami's plan to show Lucy a beautiful holiday weekend in lieu of seducing her—*that* was the problem.

It wasn't working. It had been a bad plan from its very inception. Less than twenty-four hours ago he'd been so sure he could never find her physically attractive. She'd shot down that certainty in the space of an afternoon.

After that chaste kiss at the harbor, he'd known he had a problem.

And how had he dealt with that problem? Why, by kissing her again that night, at which time his body had actively responded to the taste of her mouth and the feel of her pressed against him, filling his arms. He was as bad as old Dietrich VonDelft, sniffing around after an innocent who had a right to learn about love from someone as sweet and untried as she was.

"Luce," he began severely, despising the stiff, stuffy sound of his own voice, "I have something I really must say to you."

Instantly, her face changed. Her mouth went soft

and her brown eyes went stormy. "Oh, no. What is it? What's the matter now?"

"I've been, er, reconsidering this situation, meaning this weekend, you and me, together."

She made a small unhappy sound. "Reconsidering? Why?"

"We have to be realistic."

"What? But I *am* realistic. I promise you, I am."

"I'm only saying that on second thought, it's a bad idea."

She gulped. "A bad idea…?"

"Think about it. Where can it go, really? Have you sat down and honestly considered how you'll feel if we spend a night together? Have you given any thought to what would happen next?"

She blinked. "Omigod. You're worried about the same thing Noah's afraid of. That you'll hurt me. That you'll break my heart." And then she turned her elfin face away and slid him the most endearing sideways glance. "You *are* worried about that, aren't you?"

How did she do that? Get him at a disadvantage with simple honesty and a sideways look? "I'm your friend, Luce."

"I know that. Of course you are."

"I'm your friend and I want you to have so much. I want you to have what you need. And what a lovely young woman needs is a young man as eager and hopeful and…pure at heart as she."

"Oh, no." She shook a finger at him. "Oh, Dami. Really. I told you. I'm totally behind the curve on this. I need someone to *teach* me, to bring me up to speed. I don't have time to be fumbling around with some guy who's as inexperienced as I am—and as far as your hurting me, your breaking my heart... Can't you see? I'm not like that. Not like most inexperienced girls."

"But you *are* inexperienced. And it's wrong for me to take advantage of you."

"Take advantage? No, that is not what you're doing. You would be doing me a favor. A very special kind of favor."

"No."

"Yes! You and Noah, you're both so afraid I'm going to get my heart broken. But see, my heart was broken for most of my life. Yeah, okay, it was technically a birth defect that caused a faulty valve. But it made me different, made me feel I would never have all the things everyone else takes for granted. I always tried to put a smiling face on it, but deep down my heart was broken for all the life I would never have."

"But now you're well," he reminded her, preparing to go on and explain calmly and gently how she only had to be a little patient. She would meet someone special and nature would take it from there.

But before he could say that, she went right on. "Exactly. I'm well. New techniques were developed and I had the surgery I needed, finally." She put a hand to her breast. "My heart is now *un*broken. And yeah, okay, I might be hurt by a man, by love gone wrong. I might suffer the way any woman suffers when she loses the guy who matters most. But even if that happened, so what? That's what real life is. Being hurt, getting up and going on. And maybe, if you're richly blessed, finding true happiness in time. I'm up for that. For whatever happens. Because my heart is *un*broken and now I'm strong enough to see a heartache through to the happiness on the other side."

Damien stared at her. How could he help himself?

She really was amazing. He could just sit there and listen to her chatter away, waving her pretty hands, saying things that touched him, things that made him feel glad simply to know her, to be her friend.

But he had to do the right thing by her. He had to make her see the light. "That's just it. It all becomes convoluted and complex between men and women when sex enters into it. It's rarely as simple as you might want it to be—especially when it's your first time."

"I see that, I do. That's why I chose you. Because you do love me." He must have winced, because she added quickly, "Settle down. Take a deep breath. I mean as a dear friend. You love me and I love you and you have always shown such care for me. Noah wants me to be safe. And you know what? With you, I will be. I have no doubt of that. I will be safe and treated right. And when it's over, I swear to you, I will smile at you and wish you the best of everything and let you go."

Damn it to the depths of hell. What could he possibly say to that?

Not that it mattered what he might have said, because of course Lucy was still talking. "Tell me the truth," she demanded, biting her soft lower lip.

"Er…which truth is that?"

She gave him another of those sweet sideways glances. "Remember when you kissed me in my room earlier?"

As though he could possibly forget. "What are you getting at?"

"You…liked it, didn't you?"

He opened his mouth to tell her a lie—and nothing came out.

She shook that finger at him again. "Dami, I may be inexperienced, but I saw the look on your face. I felt your arms around me. I felt…everything. I know that you liked kissing me. You liked it and that made you realize that you *could* make love with me after all. That you could do it and even enjoy it. And that wasn't what you meant to do when you told me we could have the weekend together. That ruined your plan—the plan I have been totally up on right from the first—your plan to show me a nice time and send me back to America as ignorant of lovemaking as I was when I got here."

"Luce…"

"Just answer the question, please."

"I have absolutely no idea what the question was."

"Did you like kissing me?"

Now he was the one gulping like some green boy. "Didn't *you* already answer that for me?"

"I did, yeah. But I would also like to have you answer it for yourself."

He wanted to get up and walk out of the room. But more than that, he wanted what she kept insisting *she* wanted. He wanted to take off her floppy sweater, her skinny jeans and her pink canvas shoes. He wanted to see her naked body. And take her in his arms. And carry her to his bed and show her all the pleasures she was so hungry to discover.

"Dami. Did you like kissing me?"

"Damn you," he said, low.

And then she said nothing. That shocked the hell out of him. Lucy. Not saying a word. Not waving her hands around. Simply sitting there with her big sweater drooping off one silky shoulder, daring him with her eyes to open his mouth and tell her the truth.

He never could resist a dare. "Yes, Luce. I did. I liked kissing you. I liked it very much."

A small pleased gasp escaped her. She clapped her

hands. "Then there's no problem. It's all going to work out. We'll have our weekend. We'll see how it goes." God, she was something extraordinarily fine. So eager and lovely, her eyes shining with anticipation at the possible pleasures to come.

And who did he think he was fooling? He was who he was. When confronted with temptation, he inevitably found a way to surrender to it. She was right. He knew that he wanted her now, and that changed everything.

He only prayed that when it ended, he could still be her friend.

Chapter Five

Five hours later Damien sat across from her at a small round corner table in his favorite café, a narrow window-fronted shop on a side street in the mostly residential ward of La Cacheron.

"I love it here," Lucy declared. She was looking amazing, as usual, in a short ruffled skirt, a white schoolgirl blouse, black suede boots and a bright yellow sweater. Amazing and wonderfully young, he thought, so fresh faced and glowing after staying up most of the night battling first with her brother and then with him.

"What, exactly, do you love?" he asked, so that she would continue talking and waving her hands about.

She put out both arms to the side, palms up. "I love the black-and-white linoleum floor, the dark wood counters, the waitresses in their little white aprons, those plain shirtwaist dresses and sensible shoes. They look like they've been working here all their lives."

"Most of them have." He sipped his café au lait and nodded at their server, Justine, who was tall and deep breasted with steel-gray hair. "Justine has been serving me since before I could walk. Gerta, our nanny, used to bring us here at least twice a week."

"Us?"

"My brothers, my sisters and me. Sometimes my mother or my father would bring us. They've always loved it here, too. The croissants are excellent and Justine and the others always knew to wait on us without a lot of fanfare so we would be comfortable and able to enjoy just being a family out for a treat."

She ate the last bite of her croissant. "Um. So good." A flaky bit of pastry clung to her plump lower lip.

He imagined leaning across and licking it off. "Finish your coffee," he said a little more gruffly than he meant to.

She dabbed at her lip with her napkin and then sipped her coffee slowly. "Are we in a rush?"

"We don't want to miss the Procession of Abundance."

"Ah, yes," she answered airily. "I read the guidebook. It's an age-old Montedoran tradition that always occurs on a Friday at the end of November. A parade of farmers and vintners marching the length of the principality to the Cathedral of Our Lady of Sorrows in order to have their seeds and vines blessed, thus ensuring bountiful crops in the year to come."

He nodded approval. "Very good. But don't forget the donkeys."

She pressed a hand, fingers spread, across her upper chest. "I can't believe I forgot the donkeys. The farmers and vintners all ride on donkeys."

He gave another nod. "As did our Lord on Palm Sunday and Mary on the way to Bethlehem, the donkey symbolizing loyalty and humility and the great gift of peace, which brings the possibility of abundance. Ready to go?"

She set down her white stoneware cup. "I just want to look at the pictures first." And she swept out her left arm to indicate the sketches and paintings that jostled for space on the dark wood-paneled walls. A moment later she was up and strolling the length of the shop, her gaze scanning the framed oils, watercolors and pencil drawings created by local artists over the years.

He left the money on the table and got up and went with her. She stopped opposite three drawings grouped together on the back wall. One was a street view of the café's front window, one of a slightly younger Justine, in profile, bending to set a cup on a table. The third was the front window again but seen from inside. A fat cat sat on the window ledge looking out.

Lucy said, "I do like these three. The cat reminds me of Boris." Boris was her fat orange tabby.

"Is Boris still in California?" When he'd taken her to New York, they'd had to leave Boris behind in the care of Hannah Russo, Lucy's former foster mother, who was now Noah's housekeeper.

Lucy shook her head, her gaze on the cat in the drawing. "Hannah brought him to me a few weeks ago. He likes it in Manhattan. He sits in the front window and watches all the action down on the street—very much like this cat right here." He knew she'd already checked for and found the scrawled initials, DBC, in the lower left-hand corners of each of the sketches. Lucy was always after him to dedicate more of his time to painting and drawing. She added, "These are so good, Dami. When did you do them?"

He slid his arm around her waist, allowing himself the small, sharp pleasure of touching her, of feeling the warmth of her beneath the softness of her cashmere cardigan with its prim row of white buttons down the front. "Years ago. I was studying briefly at Beaux-Arts in Paris and drawing everything in sight. I came in for coffee, had my sketchbook with me. Justine gave me a box of pastries in exchange for these."

She leaned into him a little. He caught the scents of coffee and vanilla—and peaches. Today she smelled of peaches. And she scolded, as he'd known she would, "You should spend more time drawing and painting."

It was delicious, the feel of her against his side. "Life is full of diversions and there aren't enough hours in a day."

"Still…"

He turned her toward the door. "Let's go. The Procession of Abundance won't wait."

After the parade, they strolled the Promenade in the harbor area, not far from where he'd told stories to the children the day before.

She chattered gleefully about her upcoming first semester at the Fashion Institute of New York. She'd been to the school and pestered some of her future instructors for ways she might better prepare for the classes to come. As a result, she was designing accessories and working with fabrics she hadn't used before.

And then, again, she brought up his painting. "I know you have a studio here in Montedoro. I want you to take me there."

He teased, "Never trust a man who wants to show you his etchings."

"But that's just it. You *don't* want to show me. You keep putting me off."

He took her soft, clever hand and tucked it over his arm. "I'll consider it."

She bumped her shoulder against him and flashed him a grin. "And I'll keep bugging you until you give in and let me see what you've been working on."

"But I haven't been working on any of that. I'm a businessman first. And you know that I am."

"You're an artist, Dami," she insisted. "You truly are."

"No, my darling. *You* are. Now please stop nagging me or I won't take you to the holiday gala at the National Museum tonight."

Her big eyes got wider. "Oh, that's right. I'd almost forgotten about the show at the museum. There will be an exhibit of that new car you've been working on, the Montedoro, won't there?"

"You make it sound as though I built the car personally."

She put on an expression of great superiority. "I know how to use the internet, believe it or not. I read all about the new sports car and how you helped design it."

"So, then, we're agreed."

She sent him a look. "Agreed about what?"

"You'll go with me to the gala tonight. We'll drink champagne. I will dazzle you with my knowledge of Montedoran art. And you'll stop giving me grief about how I should spend more time in my studio."

Lucy wore red to the gala that night. Her own design, the dress was strapless, of red satin, with a mermaid hem and a giant jeweled vintage pin in the shape of a butterfly at the side of her waist. She felt good in that dress—comfortable and about as close to glamorous as someone everyone considered "cute" was ever going to get.

Dami said, "Wow," when he saw it. And she had to admit, the way he looked at her, all smoldering and sexy, had her convinced that the dress was just right.

The National Museum of Montedoro filled a very old, very large rococo-style villa perched on a hillside overlooking the harbor. Dami's sister Rhiannon, who was a year older than Alice, worked there. Rhia oversaw acquisitions and restorations. She greeted the guests as they entered the museum.

Seven months pregnant, wearing royal-blue satin, Rhia had that glow that so many pregnant women get. She kissed Lucy on the cheek and said that Alice and Noah were expected any minute now. Lucy shared a glance with Dami over that. He frowned a little, probably doubting that Noah would behave himself. Lucy flashed him a confident smile. Noah would behave himself, all right. If he didn't, he'd get another middle-of-the-night visit from his little sister.

Rhia said, "Follow the Hall of Tapestries. The Montedoro Exhibit is in the South Gallery. You can't miss it."

They proceeded down a long hallway hung with beautiful tapestries, some of them very old, to a large two-story room with tall windows overlooking the harbor. The second floor was a balcony rimming the space. Guests could stand at the railing up there and gaze down on the action below.

The gallery was already milling with people in full evening dress sipping champagne. A jazz quartet played on a stage near the windows. A sleek red sports car gleamed under spotlights in the center of the room.

"It's so beautiful," she told Dami at the sight of the new car.

"It has to be," he said. "After all, it's called the Montedoro."

They made their way around the exhibit. Lucy took her time, studying the photographs and scale drawings and reading the descriptions that detailed the creation of the new car. The Montedoro would be available to exclusive individual buyers that coming May and offered for sale in upscale auto dealerships all over the world in the fall. Many of the drawings were signed DBC.

Evidently, Dami saw her checking out his initials. "See? There's more to life than painting and sketching fat cats in windows."

"Noah told me that you took a degree in mechanical engineering and design."

"I like to keep busy."

"You're way too modest."

"Oh, no, I'm not." He leaned closer and his warm breath brushed her temple. "I have a lot of interests. And I become bored very easily."

"You hide your abilities behind your jet-setter facade."

"Does anyone actually say *jet-setter* anymore?"

She drew her shoulders back. "I do. It's a perfect way of saying shallow-rich-people-who-fly-all-over-the-place-in-their-private-jets. Just IMO, of course."

He pretended to hide a yawn. "I hope this isn't the beginning of one of your lectures concerning my wasted artistic talent. I thought we had an understanding about that."

"You're right." She did her best to look contrite. "We do. And I didn't mean to insult rich people with too much time on their hands."

"As opposed to hardworking rich people, you mean?"

"Well, you have to admit, a hardworking rich person is much more admirable."

"Spoken like an American."

She scolded, "And would you please stop telling me how easily you get bored?"

He leaned even closer and whispered, "Done."

She breathed him in. He did smell wonderful. "Terrific."

He touched her hair, tracing the line of it along her temple and cheek then following the shell of her ear. A little shiver of pleasure went through her and he whispered, "Not bored now. Not with you…."

They were sharing a lovely, intimate smile when she heard the disturbance by the wide arch that opened back onto the Hall of Tapestries. Dami was facing the entrance. He could see what was happening. His tender look turned to a scowl. Lucy followed his gaze to the stunning woman surrounded by admirers and eager photographers just entering the exhibit.

It was Vesuvia.

And she looked even more magnificent than she did on the covers of all those glamorous fashion magazines, with magnetic almond-shaped eyes, cheekbones to die for and lips so full they should be X-rated. She was very tall, with shapely shoulders and long, graceful arms. Her lion's mane of tawny hair fell to the middle of her back and her perfect round breasts seemed to defy gravity. She wore a low-cut white gown that clung lovingly to every curve and was slit high on the right side to reveal a whole lot of toned golden-skinned leg and a pair of Grecian-inspired metallic sandals with the straps wrapping halfway up her otherworldly calves. She laughed and tossed her acres of hair and the photographers went into a frenzy of picture taking, calling encouragements to her and begging, "Vesuvia, this way!" and "Vesuvia, over here!"

Dami leaned close again, "Don't stare, Luce. It only encourages her."

Lucy turned back to him, feeling slightly dazed, the way you do when you stare directly into the sun. "Sorry, Dami. How can I help it? She's pretty amazing to look at, you know?" She glanced again at his ex-girlfriend just as the woman raised her golden arm to send Dami a little wave, a come-and-get-me smile on those impossibly large lips. And that had Lucy whipping her head back to catch Dami's reaction.

But his gaze was waiting for her. "You look as though you're watching a tennis match."

She didn't deny it. "Am I?"

"Not on my part. I've conceded that game."

Are you sure? she longed to ask. But no. Maybe later when they were alone, if it felt right, they might talk about his ex. Because they were friends and they trusted each other.

But to get into all that now, well, uh-uh. Time and place, it wasn't. Plus, Lucy found she felt… Well, not jealous, exactly. How could she be jealous? She and Dami didn't have that kind of thing going on.

But at a disadvantage. Yes, that was it. Like suddenly she was walking around blindfolded in an unfamiliar room, groping at the furniture, trying to find her way.

Vesuvia and her posse were headed for the scale model of the Montedoro in the center of the exhibit. A man and a woman broke from the group. The woman wore a black sheath cocktail dress and the man a dark suit. Both had on ear-to-ear smiles. They came right for Lucy and Damien.

"Watch out," Dami warned. "Ad executives." He named a major international advertising company.

"Your Highness," fawned the woman. "How *are* you?"

Dami nodded. "Wonderful to see you." He introduced Lucy. She murmured a hello.

The woman gave her a quick nod and got right to the point. "I wonder, a few pictures? You and Vesuvia and the Montedoro? Is it possible, do you think?"

"Of course," he said. "I'll be right over."

The man said, "Excellent."

The woman said, "Perfect."

And then they both turned and went back to where Vesuvia was laughing and tossing her head in front of the red car.

Dami wrapped an arm around Lucy's shoulder, drew her close to his side and spoke softly in her ear. "We want to keep the Montedoro in the news. Unfortunately, that means I have to try to say yes to any and all shameless photo ops whenever the car happens to be involved."

Lucy didn't like it. And it annoyed her that she didn't like it. She kind of did feel jealous after all. Ugh. Jealousy was not in her plan.

Dami did the loveliest thing then. He pressed his lips against her hair, just above her right ear. "Luce? Are you all right?"

Really, she had to stop crushing on him. It just wasn't fair, wasn't part of their arrangement. She put on a bright voice. "Of course. I get it." And she did. He and Vesuvia might or might not be through, but pictures of them together would fuel rumors about them and their stormy relationship. The pictures would make all the tabloids—and the Montedoro would be in all the pictures. "Go ahead with your photo op. I'm just going to look around the other exhibits a little."

He pulled her close again and pressed a kiss to her forehead. His lips were warm and soft and a thrill went through her. She felt the affection in that brushing caress. At the same time, she couldn't help thinking, *Oh, Dami. On the forehead? Way to make me feel like a child.*

Still, she met his eyes one more time and smiled like she didn't have a care in the world. And then she left him so he could go and pose with his ex.

She headed for the Hall of Tapestries, trotting as fast as her mermaid hem would allow, determined to make a quick escape from the South Gallery. But she wasn't quite quick enough. As she passed under the wide arch that got her out of there, she spotted Noah and Alice coming straight for her.

They saw her. What else could she do but deal with them? If she took off running, Noah would assume there must be something bothering her. And then when he got into the gallery and saw Dami and Vesuvia together, he would guess what that something was.

He might get mad about it in his protective big-brother way. Or he might just feel sorry for her because she'd been crushing on Dami and look where that had gotten her. Neither of those possibilities was acceptable. Okay, maybe she wasn't gorgeous and sophisticated with perfect breasts and legs for days. She had other things going for her. Among them her pride.

No way Noah was going to see her suffering over Dami—not that she *was* suffering over Dami. She wasn't.

Not much, anyway.

She waited, smiling sweetly, as they approached her.

And then she stood there for five full minutes chatting with them, telling them how impressed she was with the car Dami had helped to design and how she couldn't wait to check out more of the museum.

Then Noah said, "Where is Damien, anyway?"

She gestured back toward the gallery behind her. "Major photo op with Vesuvia."

Alice said, "That's right, Vesuvia's the spokesmodel for the Montedoro." She lowered her voice to a just-between-us level. "They signed her for the job before she and Dami got completely on the outs."

Completely on the outs. That sounded kind of good— not that it was anything Dami hadn't already told her.

About then, Rule, who was second-born of Damien's brothers, came toward them with his wife, Sydney. Alice waved them over. Lucy was able to say a quick hello to the prince and his wife and then move on. She tried to go with dignity and slow steps, her head high.

The Hall of Tapestries took her back to the grand entry in the center of the villa. Rooms and other hallways branched off the entry like the spokes of a wheel. A curving staircase soared up behind the information desk. The main directory told her there were three stories of galleries to explore.

She began with the north wing on the ground floor, in the three galleries dedicated to textiles and clothing. First off, she found a gallery full of beautiful examples of Montedoran clothing through the years. There was an excess of what she thought of as the Little Dutch Girl look—blousy homespun shirts with snug lace-up bodices worn over them and full embroidered skirts, layers of lacy petticoats beneath and frilly aprons on top.

The next room had the finery that the princely family had worn. The exhibit spanned hundreds of years, with examples of clothing worn by many generations of the Calabretti family. The gowns were spectacular, some of them sewn with pearls and semiprecious stones. The lacework, even yellowed with age, stole her breath.

The wedding gown was there, the one Princess Adrienne had worn when she'd married Dami's dad. Lucy had been drooling over pictures of that famous dress long before she was old enough to hold a needle and thread. The gown held pride of place in the center of the exhibit, in a tall glass case. Lucy stood and stared at it for a long time.

It really lifted her spirits to see it close up, the impossibly perfect embroidery, the exquisite lace, the thousands of sewn-on seed pearls. Looking at Princess Adrienne's wedding dress reminded her of the great adventure that lay before her as a designer. It made her remember that her life was rich and full and good. That she was *not* going to be jealous of Dami and his ex— or if she was, a little, it was okay. Even the unpleasant emotions were part of being alive and she would take life over the alternative any day of the week.

Warm hands clasped her waist. Dami. "How did I know I would find you here?"

She'd been so transported by the legendary wedding dress that she hadn't seen his faint reflection in the glass of the protective case. But she saw him now. She turned to him and brought her palms up to rest on the satin lapels of his jacket. "I can now say I've seen *the dress* in person. Not to mention generations' worth of serious Calabretti style. I've also already checked out the various examples of traditional Montedoran dress."

He still held her waist and his eyes gleamed down at her. "Are you saying you're ready to move on?"

She hooked her arm in his. "Where to next?"

He took her back to the main entrance and up the stairs to the Adele Canterone Exhibit. For an easy, companionable hour they admired the art of Montedoro's great Impressionist painter.

They ran into Noah and Alice again on the way out.

Alice said, "Come back to the villa with us, you two. We'll share a late supper."

Lucy instantly suspected that Noah might be up to something. She gave him a long narrow-eyed look.

Noah was all innocence. "What? Good company, something to eat. Is that going to kill you?"

Lucy couldn't help grinning. "Fine." She glanced at Dami, who nodded in agreement. "We would love to come." Then she teased her brother. "Because I can see you're on your best behavior."

Noah made a growly sound. "Do I have a choice?"

And Alice answered sweetly, "No, you do not."

So they went to the villa and shared a light supper, the four of them. Overall, it went pretty well, Lucy thought. Noah and Dami seemed fine with each other. If there was tension between them, it didn't show. They talked about Montedoro and also about some business deal they were working on together.

And the coolest thing happened just as they were leaving.

Alice took her aside. "I know you're going to be busy with school and everything. But is it possible you might be able to design my wedding dress? It's just the design I would need, by mid-February if you can manage it. Then I'll have it made."

Lucy grabbed her and spun her around and they laughed together. "Are you kidding? I can do that. And absolutely, yes. I would be totally honored—and do you have ideas about what you want?"

"A thousand of them. I'm counting on you to focus me down."

Then Noah butted in, wrapping an arm around Lucy. "When you come home for Christmas, you two can get to work on it."

Noah knew very well that she planned to stay in New York for the holiday. Still, he'd been a sweetheart all night, so she made an effort to answer patiently. "Noah, we've been over that. I'm having my first Christmas in my own place, remember?"

He opened his mouth to start telling her all the reasons she really needed to come to California.

But Alice grabbed his arm, pulled him close and kissed his cheek. "I love you. Shut up."

And miracle of miracles, Noah actually did shut up. And he did it without looking the least pissed off.

Damien had a car waiting at the curb outside the villa. They rode back to the palace in comfortable silence.

He was having a great time. Being with Lucy really worked for him. She saw beauty in everything and she wasn't afraid to let her enjoyment show.

He couldn't help comparing her to V, who'd been just next door to manic during the photo op. All flashing eyes and flying hair, hanging on him for the cameras, she'd hissed in Italian that she was furious at him for not taking her calls. She'd sworn she'd never forgive him. He'd reminded her softly that it was over. She'd given him a melting look for the photographers' sake while calling him any number of unflattering names under her breath. All he could think of was getting the hell away from her.

As it turned out, Lady Luck had his back on that

score. The ad people had said they wanted a few more shots just with V and the car. He'd slipped away. And things had improved dramatically when he found Luce in the north wing of the museum, gazing with stars in her eyes at his mother's wedding gown.

A few minutes after they left Alice's villa, they arrived at the palace. A guard let them in.

Dami said, "I'll walk you up to your room."

And she took his arm and begged so prettily, "Please. Can't we just go to your apartment and talk for a little while?"

It wasn't a good idea. He knew that. True, in the darkest hours of the morning before, he'd been weak, he'd indulged himself and imagined that becoming her lover was inevitable.

But he'd had time to see the light since then. She mattered too much to him. He couldn't bear to lose her. If he took her to bed, there would be bad feelings when it was time to move on. Someone would be bound to get hurt. Someone always did.

Therefore, he'd circled back around to his original plan. He would show her a memorable weekend, minus the part where they ended up in bed together. She understood that their making love wasn't a given. She'd said it herself: they would see how it went. He planned to see to it that it went nowhere.

"Dami." She tugged on his arm. "What *are* you thinking about?"

He studied her fabulous elfin face. "That you remind me of a princess from a Montedoran fairy tale."

She colored prettily. "Thank you." And then she commanded, "Take me to your apartment."

He opened his mouth to remind her that it had been a

long day, but somehow what came out was, "Yes, Your Highness. This way...."

In his rooms, they went straight to the kitchen. She asked for hot chocolate. He made it the way they did in Paris, chopping bars of fine-quality bittersweet chocolate and whisking the bits into the heated milk, stirring in brown sugar and a few grains of sea salt.

She admired the Limoges demitasse and sipped slowly. "Dami. Your hot chocolate is even better than your coffee."

He poured himself a cup and sat down opposite her.

And she said, "I probably shouldn't admit this. It will only prove all over again how gauche and immature I am...."

He set down his cup. "You're not. Admit what?"

She sucked her upper lip between her neat white teeth, then caught herself doing it and let it go. "When you went to pose for those pictures with Vesuvia?"

"Yes?"

"I actually got jealous."

As a rule, when any woman mentioned jealousy, he tended to get nervous, to feel hemmed in, under pressure. But with Lucy he only felt flattered at her frankness. And a little bit guilty for deserting her. "I shouldn't have left you...."

"Oh, don't you dare apologize. You didn't do anything wrong— Well, except when you kissed me on the forehead. That made me feel about five."

"It was a kiss of affection."

"I know. Still. Five."

"Fair enough, then. No more kisses on the forehead."

"Cheek, temples, ears, lips... Well, just about anywhere is great. But not smack-dab in the middle of my forehead."

Kissing her just about anywhere sounded way too appealing, and he probably shouldn't be thinking about that. "All right. Not on the forehead." He found he needed to be sure she had it clear about V. "And about V?"

She was midsip. She swallowed fast and set down the cup, big eyes getting bigger. "Yeah?"

"Nothing to be jealous of. I meant it when I told you that Vesuvia and I are over."

She turned the painted gold-rimmed cup on the delicate saucer. And then she sipped again. "You were, um, exclusive with her for quite a while."

"Yes."

"But you have such a rep as a player, as someone who never makes it exclusive with any woman...."

"I was exclusive with V."

"Why?"

He looked into his cup of chocolate and then back up at her. "You are *very* nosy."

She nodded, a sweet bobbing motion of her pretty head. "Yes. I am. I know. But only because I'm your friend and I want to understand you better."

He believed her. And so he explained, "When I met V, I was looking for the right wife. I wanted someone suited to me. At first V behaved reasonably for the most part. She's bright and beautiful. I thought we could make it work together. I was attracted to her."

"You loved her."

"Love wasn't really the issue."

"But when you get married, love is *always* the issue."

He gave her his most patient look. "No, Luce. Not always."

"So then why did you choose her?"

"I found her attractive and intelligent. I thought we

had a lot in common. She's descended from a very old Italian family. We know many of the same people. I never proposed marriage to her, but V understood that I needed to marry and she told me more than once that she wanted to be my wife, to be a princess of Montedoro."

"You *needed* to marry? Why?"

He'd assumed she knew. Apparently not. "You haven't heard of the Prince's Marriage Law?" She shook her head, so he explained, "The Prince's Marriage Law decrees that all princes of Montedoro are required to marry by the age of thirty-three or be stripped of all titles and relieved of the large fortune they each inherit by virtue of their birth."

She made a low sound in her throat. "Well, that's just wrong."

"It's a controversial law and has been abolished in the past. But then the Calabretti line almost died out. My grandfather had it reinstated."

"You'll be thirty-two in January...."

He put his hand to his heart and teased, "You remembered."

"Of course I remember. Aren't you worried you won't find the right woman?"

"But don't you see? I did worry. And I was practical. At the age of twenty-nine, with plenty of time to spare, I went looking for a bride. And you can see how well that went."

"Not well at all."

"So I'm becoming more philosophical about it. What will happen will happen."

"Dami," she scolded, "it's your inheritance...."

Now he looked at her sternly. "I'm fully aware of

that. You are not to worry about it. It's not your concern."

She was quiet. But only for a moment. "So, then, you're telling me that Vesuvia didn't love you, either. She just wanted to be a princess."

"And that was all right with me. I needed a suitable bride. She liked the idea of marrying a prince."

"Oh, Dami. You sound so cynical."

"Because I *am* cynical."

"No, you're not. Not in your heart."

He chuckled. "Go ahead. Believe wonderful things about me if you must."

"Thank you. I will." She leaned toward him, all eyes. "What changed your mind about proposing to her?"

"At first, as I said, she behaved reasonably. But she didn't *stay* reasonable, because at heart she's *not* reasonable. In the end, it's always a big drama with V. She can't just...sit at a table and talk, over cocoa." He watched her smile, only a hint of one, a slight lifting at the corner of her tender mouth. "With V there must be grand gestures, and often. She craves expensive gifts and constant attention. She loves to stage a big dramatic scene. I can't count the number of times she walked out on me in restaurants after telling me off in very colorful Italian."

"Whew. Yeah. I can see how that would get pretty old after a while."

"It's been over for months now, really. At least, as far as I'm concerned."

"Not for her, though?"

"Let me put it this way. I'm through. I've told her I'm through. She says she understands and then she starts calling again."

"So maybe she loves you after all. Maybe she *still* loves you...."

"Luce, it's not love. Believe me."

She reached across the table and put her soft hand over his. "You look so sad, Dami."

Sad? Was he? "My parents married for love."

"Oh, yeah." She squeezed his hand. Her touch felt so good. "They're, like, legendary, your parents. The American actor and the Montedoran princess, finding true love, living happily ever after...."

With his thumb, he idly stroked the back of her hand—until he realized he was doing it and released her. She gave the tiniest shrug, pulled her arm back to her side of the table and slowly ran a finger around the rim of her demitasse. He thought about kissing her— and not on the forehead.

And what were they talking about?

His parents. Right. "Growing up, we all—my brothers and sisters and I—loved what they had. We all knew we wanted to grow up and have that kind of love for ourselves. Well, except for my twin, Alex. Alex was always...separate. Alone. But in the end, he found his way to Lili. He found true love after all. That's what we do, we Bravo-Calabrettis. We marry for love. We mate for life. Of the nine of us, only my youngest sisters, Genny and Rory, haven't found the one for them yet. They have plenty of time. They're both in their early twenties—like you."

"And what about you, Dami? You haven't found the one." She regarded him solemnly. "I hope you do."

He thought how perceptive she was, really, for someone so young. Once, Alice had told him that Lucy was more grown-up than he realized. He hadn't believed her at the time. But he was beginning to see he'd been wrong.

"Dami?"

He gave a low laugh. It was a sound without much humor. "No, I haven't found 'the one.' I honestly believe now that I'm the exception who proves the family rule. I enjoy the thrill of a new romance. I can't get enough of the chase. But I don't have what it takes for a lifetime of happiness with one woman."

"Oh, come on." She cast a glance at the ceiling and gestured grandly with both hands, the way she liked to do. "So it didn't work out with Vesuvia. You know what Hannah would say?"

He put on a pained expression. "Don't tell me. Please."

Lucy only grinned. She was very fond of her former foster mother. "Hannah would say, get over yourself. Try again. Forget finding someone *suitable*—look for someone to love. And choose a nicer woman this time."

"Nice women bore me—present company excluded, of course."

She fluttered her eyelashes. "Good save."

"I *am* the Player Prince after all. It's my job to be smooth."

She drank the last of her cocoa. "That was so good it had to be sinful." Then she pushed her chair back and stood.

He gazed up the length of her, taking in the pretty curves of her bare shoulders and the brave beauty of that inch of scar tissue her gown didn't hide. "Did I tell you that you are incomparable in red?"

She dimpled at him. "It never hurts to say something like that more than once."

"You're very fine, Luce. Absolutely splendid." His

pulse had accelerated and his breath came faster. Warning signs, he knew. Temptation was calling again and the urge to surrender becoming more insistent.

He knew what to do: move, get up, break the sweet spell of this breath-held moment. Stop thinking that he wanted her more today than yesterday, more now than an hour ago, more in this minute than the minute before.

And what was he doing, anyway, keeping on with this, with her? If he wasn't going to take her to bed, he needed to stay away from her.

But he wasn't willing to do that. He wanted this time with her as much as she seemed to want it with him.

The truth skittered through him, striking off sparks: he didn't want to stop. And he wasn't going to stop.

Impossible. Sweet Lucy Cordell, of all people. He never would have imagined. Not in a hundred years.

But he imagined it now, in detail. With growing excitement. In spite of her brother's probable fury. Even if it ended up costing him her friendship.

Really, he ought to be a better man. Unfortunately, he wasn't.

She stepped away from her chair, pushed it in and came around the table toward him in a rustle of red satin, her eyes never letting go of his, all woman in that moment, the girl he had known before eclipsed, changed. When she stood above him, she reached down and put her hand on his shoulder.

Her touch burned him, made his throat clutch, tangled his breath inside his suddenly aching chest. He couldn't bear it. He caught her fingers, brought them to his mouth, pressed the tips of them against his lips. Heat seared his belly and tightened his groin. She sucked in a sharp breath. He kissed her fingers one more time and then let go.

That was when she said so sweetly, "Stand up, Dami. Please."

Chapter Six

Damien rose and stood with her and tried to think what to say. "Luce…"

She lifted on tiptoe, so her sweet mouth was so wonderfully, perfectly close. Her breath smelled of cocoa. "I haven't had a lot of kisses. I mean, real kisses. On-the-lips kisses."

He whispered her name again. "Luce." Somehow her name was the only word he had right then.

She continued on the subject of kisses. "Two from you, so far. Two from a boy I met in Cardiac ICU at a very excellent hospital in Los Angeles. His name was Ramon. He was getting better, they said. And then one night, out of nowhere, he died. He had the most beautiful crow-black hair." A single tear escaped the corner of her left eye.

He dipped his head, kissed that tear, tasted the salty wetness on his tongue.

She drew in a shaky little breath, put her hands on his shoulders as though bracing herself—and continued, "A boy named Troy kissed me in middle school. It was one of the few times I was well enough to go to school for a while. He kissed me out under the football bleachers. I promised to meet him in front of the school in the morning. But I got bad in the night and there was another surgery and I didn't go to school again for three years."

He made a low noise in his throat, a noise of encouragement, and he pressed his lips to the pretty arch of her left eyebrow.

She went on, "And then there was this boy in high school, a very pricey private school. I went there for three months in my junior year. Noah was rich by then...."

Her brother had started from nothing. Lucy's illnesses had spurred him on to greater and greater success. He'd needed a lot of money to make sure she got the very best care available.

Lucy went on. "The boy in high school? His name was Josh and he lived in our neighborhood in Beverly Hills— This was before Noah bought the estate in Carpinteria. Josh took me to the homecoming dance and I kissed him at the door when he brought me home. He never called me after that. I called him twice, left messages with his mom. And then a few weeks later, there I was in an ambulance again. I was homeschooled exclusively after that. I never saw Josh again and I never kissed anyone else until last year."

"You had a boyfriend last year?" He hadn't known.

"Uh-uh. It was at one of Noah's parties. A man named David, a business associate of Noah's. David would have done more than kiss me, but I got cold feet—and don't you dare tell Noah."

"Never." He growled the word and tried to recall if he'd ever met this David. He didn't think so, which was probably just as well.

"Promise me," she whispered.

"I swear on the blue blood of my Calabretti ancestors, on the honor of all the Bravos who came before me, that I will never tell Noah that you kissed a man named David at one of Noah's parties."

"Wow. Now, *that's* a vow."

"I'm so glad you approve."

She gave him her best Mona Lisa smile. "But you need to seal it with a kiss."

He didn't even hesitate. There was no point. He accepted that now. Unless she called a halt, he was in. All the way. He bent and captured her mouth, tasted chocolate and heat and a sweet, slow sigh.

She wrapped her arms around his neck and swayed closer. He felt the giving softness of her breasts against his chest. Not the least childish, the softness of those breasts. "Dami…"

He pulled her closer still, not even caring anymore that she might feel him unfurling against her belly. He only went on kissing her, dipping his tongue into the moist heat beyond her parted lips, sharing her breath, the world a wonderful place that smelled of peaches and chocolate and something else, something of Lucy, fresh and clean and womanly, too.

After a while, he lifted his head. He gazed down into those shining brown eyes.

She whispered, "That's three kisses from you. Give me another."

He drank in the sight of her flushed upturned face. "You're greedy."

"I need a lot of kisses. I've been deprived." And then she giggled.

That did it. That naughty little laugh of hers made him greedy, too. He swooped down and took her mouth again.

She cried softly, "Oh!" against his lips.

And then he kissed her long and slow and deep, sweeping a hand down to press the small of her back, pushing his hips against her, aching to have her, to feel her tight heat all around him.

She moaned a little, and she lifted her lower body up and into him. Eager. And so very sweet.

That time when he lifted his head, she took the lapels of his jacket and guided them over his shoulders. He allowed that, catching it as it fell, tossing it onto a far chair. She started on the buttons of his shirt.

He caught her hands, kissed them, one and then the other. "Anticipation is a fine thing."

She tipped her head to the side and considered. And then she blushed again. "I'm rushing it, huh?"

"I want you right now," he whispered. "I want to bury myself in you and hear you moan beneath me."

Deeper color flooded upward over her throat, her chin, her plump cheeks. Her scent intensified. "Oh. Well. Okay…"

He bent and scraped his teeth along the side of her throat.

She let out a small rough little sound and clutched him closer. "Dami…" She made his name into a plea.

He caught her earlobe between his teeth and worried it lightly. Then he whispered, "Will you be guided by me?"

Another sound escaped her, more tender than rough. She shifted her fingers up into his hair, pulling his head down into the warm woman-scented curve of her throat. "Yes. Please. That's what I want. For you to teach me."

He took her shoulders then and gently held her away from him—just enough that he could meet her wide, dazed eyes. "First of all…"

"Yes?" Breathless. Hopeful. Impossibly sweet.

"We don't have to hurry."

She groaned and then pressed her lips together.

He touched her hair. Like living silk. "Say it. Whatever you're thinking. Don't hold back."

She winced. "Well, it's just that, um, yeah, we kind of do have to hurry. I mean, it's already Saturday morning. I'm flying home tomorrow. We need to get this done."

He wanted to laugh at her total frankness, but he didn't. He held her gaze. "As your friend, I must warn you against men who say 'trust me.' But trust me."

She laughed then. "Oh, Dami."

"Do you trust me?"

She didn't hesitate. "I do. Absolutely."

"Good." He caught her hand. "Come with me."

Dazed, amazed, excited and very nervous, Lucy went where he led her.

To his bedroom.

It was a large room with a high, coffered ceiling from which hung a giant iron chandelier. The bed had an intricately carved headboard and finials shaped like crowns. The turned-back sheets were cobalt-blue satin, the bedding in deep blue and gold and red.

Unreality assailed her. Alone with Dami in his bedroom. Who knew?

He turned on a torchère lamp beside the bed nice and

low. The chandelier was on, too, but also low. She could see clearly enough, but everything was soft and shadowed. Which was great. The pleasant dimness eased her nerves.

At least a little.

He took her shoulders again, his long fingers warm and sure against her bare skin. Still, she shivered at the touch, scared and also excited for what was to come.

"Second thoughts?" he asked.

Her mouth went dust dry. She swallowed to try to get some moisture going. "No. Really. I want to do this, I truly do...."

His smile was way too knowing as he stepped back from her and began to undress, first dropping to a chair to remove his shoes and socks, then sweeping upright again and getting rid of everything else. Quickly, so gracefully, all his beautiful clothes were gone in what felt to her like an instant, as she just stood there staring.

At least the saliva had flooded back into her mouth.

He was a magnificent man, honed and tanned, with a broad, deep chest and shoulders and a belly you could scrub your laundry on. Her gaze trailed down over hard, narrow hips. The muscles in his long thighs were sharply defined. Even his feet were beautiful, long and perfectly shaped.

She did more absurd gulping as she let her glance stray upward again. This time, she allowed herself to look directly at the most private part of him. He definitely wanted her. His manhood curved up, thick and fully aroused, from the dark nest of hair between those powerful thighs.

That he wanted her was good. Excellent— Well, except for the definite largeness of him. She couldn't help it. She wondered what all virgins probably wondered.

"Seriously, Dami. Are you sure it's going to fit?" The words were out and hanging in the air between them before she stopped to think how ridiculous they would sound.

But he didn't laugh at her. He only brushed a finger slowly down the outside of her arm, bringing the goose bumps to bloom where he touched. And he said in a low rumble, "I promise you, Luce. We'll take all the time we need. You'll see. It will fit. That's how it is with men and women. We are made to fit."

"Well, of course I know that. But it's still, um… yikes. You know?"

He went very still, waiting—and watching her so closely, his eyes that strange deep black-green right then, dragonfly green. He asked, "Do you want to stop? Any time you want to stop, all you have to do is say the word."

"No. Uh-uh. I absolutely do *not* want to stop."

One corner of his sinful mouth quirked up. How did he do it? How did he stand there in front of her without a stitch on looking so comfortable in his own skin he almost didn't seem naked at all?

His finger started moving again, across the slim rolled-satin belt at her waist, pausing at the jeweled butterfly pin. He traced the shape of it and then he let his finger trail upward. He touched her breast just with that single finger. He found her nipple beneath the satin, inside the thin cup of her strapless bra. He rubbed his finger up and down until the nipple hardened.

Lucy gasped. She couldn't help it.

And then he used his thumb, too, rolling it a little, until she felt a certain flooding of heat down low, felt a thin, shimmering cord of desire forming, connecting her breast to her core. She drew another ragged breath as he moved to the other breast and repeated the process.

Then he leaned close. He licked her at her temple. The moisture made a cool spot, right there where her pulse beat above her ear.

He blew on that spot, increasing the coolness. And then he whispered, "Take off your belt...."

She did it, fumbling a little, removing the vintage pin and unhooking the clasp beneath. He took them from her and set them on the bedside table.

"Luce." He licked her temple again, caught a bit of her hair between his lips and tugged. Then he pressed his mouth to her hair. She felt his warm breath sift over her scalp. "Luce?"

"Yeah?" Her own voice sounded...different. Tentative. And breathless, too. She wished fervently to be more experienced, not to be so obviously out of her depth. Her wish was not granted.

And somehow Dami made that seem all right. "Please turn around."

She remembered to breathe again and the air rushed into her hungry lungs as she ordered her feet to move. Three careful steps and she was facing away from him, staring at the shadows in the corners of the room, at the waiting blue satin sheets on the wide carved bed.

He touched her shoulder, as though to steady her. And then he took down her zipper in one long, slow glide. The dress dropped around her ankles.

He wrapped one of those big hard arms around her and kissed the side of her neck. "Step out of it. Careful, now...." She lifted one satin stiletto and then the other, cautiously stepping free of the gown. "Don't move," he warned softly. He let go of her long enough to scoop the dress up and deposit it safely over his clothes on the bedside chair.

Then he wrapped both arms around her. He pulled her against him, his heat and hardness all along the back of her, his manhood pressing into her, making her moan, making her little red panties wet.

He cradled her breasts. It felt...so good. She let out a long sigh, and her head fell back to rest against the hard muscles of his chest. "Should I...take off my shoes?"

He kissed her ear. "No. Leave them on. There is nothing so fine as a beautiful woman in red satin shoes."

A beautiful woman. He meant *her,* Lucy. And she knew it was just Dami, just how he was. He had all the right words to make a woman want him, and he didn't hesitate to use them—and somehow when he used them, he made her believe him. He made her absolutely certain that she was every bit as beautiful and desirable as he kept saying she was.

He continued to caress her, first dipping his thumbs into the cups of her bra, easing the semisheer fabric out of the way so her breasts came free. She looked down at his big dark hands holding her breasts, rolling the nipples. At the narrow white gleam of her heart-surgery scar.

And it was so wonderfully unreal, so perfectly erotic. So totally thrilling in an otherworldly kind of way. Her hips were moving, rubbing back against him. And he kept on touching her.

Her bra fell away. She let out a small cry of surprise. He only growled low in his throat and scraped his teeth along the ridge of her shoulder, easing his mouth into the curve of her throat, sucking a little.

She brought her hand up and back, hungry to touch

him. Wrapping her fingers around his nape, she eased them up into his thick dark hair.

Time flew away. His hands were everywhere and she gloried in their knowing, hot glide over every inch of her. She had his strong, tall body at her back to steady her. And she was suddenly liquid and moving, rocking slow and loving it, as his hands moved lower, pressing at her belly, fingers easing under the elastic of her panties, finding the heart of her.

One finger drifted in where she was wet and hot and hungry. He worked such shimmering magic on her willing flesh. She was wild by then, completely outside herself. Her panties were gone, ruined—he had taken the narrow elastic on both sides and torn it so he could more easily remove them from between her shaking thighs.

And then she was naked except for her red shoes, naked with Dami, standing in front of him, her hips rocking back against his hardness, in the dim light by the wide bed.

He took her thighs and gently guided them wider, using his strong legs to support her as he did it so she didn't stumble in her high heels. And then he was *there* again, his brilliant fingers stroking her, doing the most amazing things to her wet, needful flesh. He eased one finger inside. And then another, stretching her in the most delightful, thrilling way.

And she was…riding. Riding his strong hands, riding his big body behind her. She was making such a racket, moaning and sighing. And she didn't even care. Didn't care about anything but his hardness at her back and his fingers within her. And the low words he whispered to her. Hot, wicked encouragements, praise for her heat and her wetness, her body's hunger, her greediness…

There was a light. A light that curled through her,

burning, somehow liquid. It grew outward in a widening coil. It filled her and flowed out the top of her head, streamed from her fingertips, poured through the soles of her red shoes.

And then it intensified. It was all heat and wet and it was centering down in the core of her, gathering tight where he stroked her, where he made her body open for him, open and burn.

She felt the moment. She knew it, the secret thing she'd never shared with a man before: her climax. It shuddered through her, over her, drowning her in waves of glory.

Dami stayed with her, those wonderful fingers seeming to know what to do, when to keep stroking her. And when to go still, to hold her, to press just the right spot as the pulsing became a shimmer again, a slow, lovely fade into something so perfectly, wonderfully easy and loose.

He had his arm around her waist again. And then he was turning her, scooping her up high against his chest.

She wrapped her arms around his neck and offered her mouth to him. He took it in a slow, thorough kiss as he laid her down on blue satin and then stretched out beside her, easing an arm under her head, gathering her into him, her cheek against his chest, her hand over his heart.

His lips touched her hair again, a kiss both tender and firm.

She closed her eyes for a time. The room was so quiet. His body was big and warm, her own personal heater.

When she looked again, he was watching her through eyes that were black now, limitless and so deep.

She lifted up on an elbow and gazed down at him.

He returned her look out of the center of some wonderful stillness. She marveled, "Dami, this is just how I pictured it, only better. I mean, what you did to me was so hot. And now I'm lying here naked with you in this big manly bed of yours."

"My bed is manly?" He seemed pleased.

"Oh, definitely. Yes. But the point is, it's okay, you know? You and me, naked, together. It's comfortable, easy. Good." By then she was waving the arm she wasn't leaning on. One wide sweeping gesture bopped him on the nose. "Oops."

He only laughed. "I'm glad you're happy. But please don't break my nose."

"Sorry. I promise, I'll be careful." It seemed only natural to let her hand drift lower. He was still hard. She traced the muscles of his belly—but hesitated to touch that most manly part of him. She couldn't help asking, "Does it hurt to be so big and hard?"

He gave her that beautiful half smile of his. "In a good way, yes."

"Do you need…?"

His smile went full-out. "Over the years, I find more and more pleasure in this particular sort of suffering. I enjoy the ache. I find that getting there really is a lot of the fun, that sometimes the longer it takes, the more satisfying the conclusion."

She really did want to touch it. "Is it all right if I…?"

"Yes." Gruff. Low. Like the purr of some big sleek wild animal, no less dangerous for being easy and loose, relaxing in his lair.

She explored at her leisure, loving the smooth, silky feel of his skin there, the flared mushroom shape of the head. He lay very still as she touched him and his breathing changed, becoming faster, shallower. When she bent to kiss him, he let out a low groan.

That made her smile as she lowered her mouth on him and took him inside. He whispered encouragements. She knew she wasn't doing that good of a job. But he never complained. He eased his fingers into her hair, curving them around the back of her neck as she took him in and then let him out nice and slow. He didn't try to take control. His hold was loose, gentle. And she liked that so much.

It made her feel powerful and sexy and womanly. Her mouth surrounding him, her hand wrapped around him, she was running that show.

Running it all the way to the finish, as it turned out. Beneath her hand, she felt him pulsing. His body stiffened. He let out a low, deep moan. "Luce, you should let me…"

No way. She was doing this and she was doing it right. She stayed with him, swallowed him down. He tasted like sea foam, musky and salty. He held her tighter against him right there at the end, and he growled out her name in a way that sent a hot thrill zipping through her, because she had done it, given him pleasure, just as he'd done for her.

She kissed her way up the muscular center of him, feeling naughty and bold.

He took her and turned her and tucked her against him. "Sleep."

"Huh? But we only just got started."

He chuckled. "Greedy." He sounded pleased about it.

"Dami, there's only so much time and I have so much to learn."

"Sleep," he said again.

So she closed her eyes—not for long, she told herself. Just for a little while….

When she woke, he was kissing her.

She looked down and his dark head was tracing the length of her scar as he feathered kisses along it. He kissed her breast, found another scar—a small horizontal one from years ago when she'd needed a temporary pacemaker after surgery.

He went lower. He kissed the little cluster of drainage-tube scars.

And lower still…

The things he could do with his mouth, with his tongue…

No doubt about it. She had made the right choice to come to him to get up to speed on making love.

He did it again, brought her all the way to the top of the world and then over the edge, with his mouth that time. And then he took her hand and pulled her up out of the bed and led her into the kitchen. He made them more of his delicious hot chocolate. They sat together at the table sipping cocoa without a stitch on. It was strangely erotic, like those dreams you sometimes have where you're naked someplace you would never go without your clothes on.

Once she'd finished her chocolate, he told her to get dressed, and when she had everything back on but the panties he'd torn, he said, "Now I want you to return to your room and get some sleep. I'll come for you at eleven."

"But, Dami, we haven't… I mean, it's been amazing. But we're not finished yet."

He bent close and whispered in her ear. "Don't wear any panties."

Her breath caught on a gasp. "You mean...?"

"For all day and into the evening. No panties. And don't cheat. Wear a dress or a skirt. No tights, either."

The place where her panties should have been was suddenly damp. "Oh, Dami. You are very bad."

"So I've been told. No knickers, and whenever you notice that you're without them, think of me."

Chapter Seven

All that Saturday, Lucy did think of him.

And not only because she was walking around without her panties.

How could she not think of him? He was the best friend she'd ever had, not to mention the hottest, smoothest guy she knew.

He sat across from her at another café, where they had coffee and a real breakfast. She ordered a mushroom omelet and toast with jam.

"Eat everything," he commanded. "You have to keep your strength up...." And he gave her a look. Intimate. Teasing. That look said he knew she had no knickers on. That look made promises concerning what he would do to her as soon as they were alone.

She couldn't wait, though he seemed quite happy to make her wait.

"Eat," he said again.

And she did. She ate every bite of her omelet. Both pieces of toast, too. Slathered in jam.

After that he took her where she really wanted to go: his studio, in a villa on one of the hills surrounding the harbor. He kept a flat on the lower floor. They didn't even go in there.

Upstairs in the studio, he'd had all but the load-bearing interior walls removed. His sketches and oil paintings were everywhere, some tacked to the remaining walls, some on easels or spread out on the rough worktables. It was a beautiful space, full of light even in the cool month of November. It was also chilly, though, and dusty. He turned on the heat and admitted he hadn't been there in months.

That gave her another opportunity to remind him that he should be making time for the things that mattered.

He only backed her up against a wall between a drawing of a small dark-haired girl in traditional Montedoran dress and another of a white goat chewing on a straw hat. "No lectures. Not today." And then he kissed her, a slow, lovely kiss during which he eased his clever hands inside her coat and caressed her breasts through her sweater. He also trailed his fingers up her thigh, taking her skirt along, too.

When he touched her where she wasn't wearing any panties, she moaned into his mouth as her body instantly responded. He went on touching her, stroking her. She went over the top right there while he kissed her, by the window that let in the pale late-autumn light, against the white wall.

As the fierce pleasure faded to a happy glow, she laughed and dared to put her hand down between them to feel how what he'd done to her had excited him, too. She was just running her fingers up and down the long tight bulge at his fly when the cell phone in his pocket started to vibrate.

He muttered, "Ignore it," and captured her mouth again.

But she turned away, grinning and more than a little bit breathless. "Go on, answer it—at least check and see if it's anything important."

"It's not." He bit the side of her neck and then stuck out his tongue and licked where he'd nipped her.

By then the phone had stopped its soft buzzing. She gave in and turned to him again with a willing sigh. His warm lips settled on hers.

And the phone started vibrating a second time.

He swore against her mouth—and then he lifted his head, took the phone from his pocket and switched it off quickly. But not before she saw that it was Vesuvia. He glanced up at her as he shoved it back in his pocket again and must have seen something he didn't like in her expression. "Don't *you* start in on me."

"What? I didn't—"

He stopped her from saying more by kissing her again, a long, thorough kiss, more artful than passionate. She accepted that kiss. Like all his kisses, it was too good to pass up. But the mood was pretty much trashed.

In the end, even a lover as skilled as Dami had trouble getting back into a sexy encounter after dual interruptions from the ex. He braced an arm against the wall above her shoulder and leaned his forehead against hers. "Sorry, Luce."

She tipped her head up and kissed him again, but quickly that time, brushing her lips across his. "Does she…call you a lot?"

He pushed away from the wall—and her. Impatiently,

he insisted, "It honestly is over with her, if that's what you're asking."

"I believe you. I was only…" She found she didn't know how to go on.

"What?" he demanded.

"Well, I mean, I just feel bad, that's all."

"For her?" His eyes flashed dark fire.

She held his gaze and shook her head. "No, Dami. For you. Because it didn't work out with her and I think that you really did want it to. And, well, yeah, maybe a little for her. Before he found Alice, Noah had a couple of girlfriends like that. They just wouldn't let it be, you know? They wanted more from him than he was willing to give them and they kept calling him and he was frustrated and angry and didn't know how to get through to them that over was over."

He braced his arms on the table behind him, leaned back on it and studied his fine Italian shoes. "Yes. Well, it *is* over."

"Got that. Truly." *Also that you want this subject dropped.* And really, it wasn't a bad thing for her, she thought. To be so sharply reminded of all that the beautiful man before her *wasn't* willing to give.

They had this brief magical time together. He was being so good to her, so thoughtful and tender and brilliantly instructive—not to mention very, very sexy. He was giving her what she hadn't even really understood she needed so much: to discover all the things she'd missed about passion and sex and to feel safe and cherished and free to be her whole self while it was happening.

She promised herself that tomorrow when it came time to say goodbye, she would definitely remember not

FREE Merchandise is 'in the Cards' for you!

Dear Reader,

We're giving away FREE MERCHANDISE!

Seriously, we'd like to reward you for reading this novel by giving you **FREE MERCHANDISE** worth over $20. And no purchase is necessary!

You see the Jack of Hearts sticker above? Paste that sticker in the box on the Free Merchandise Voucher inside. Return the Voucher promptly...and we'll send you valuable Free Merchandise!

Thanks again for reading one of our novels—and enjoy your Free Merchandise with our compliments!

Pam Powers

Pam Powers

P.S. Look inside to see what Free Merchandise is **"in the cards"** for you!

YOUR FREE MERCHANDISE INCLUDES...

2 FREE Harlequin® Special Edition Books
AND 2 FREE Mystery Gifts

FREE MERCHANDISE VOUCHER

2 FREE
BOOKS
and
2 FREE
GIFTS

Please send my Free Merchandise, consisting of
2 Free Books and **2 Free Mystery Gifts**.
I understand that I am under no obligation to buy
anything, as explained on the back of this card.

235/335 HDL F5J5

Please Print

FIRST NAME

LAST NAME

ADDRESS

APT.#

CITY

STATE/PROV.

ZIP/POSTAL CODE

NO PURCHASE NECESSARY!

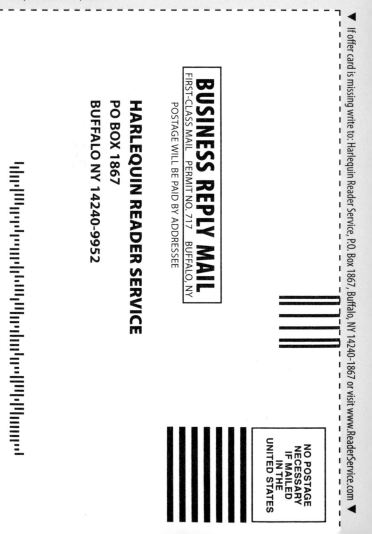

to cling. And no matter how much she wanted to hear his voice, she wouldn't start calling him all the time.

He looked up, one dark eyebrow lifted. "Shall we move on?"

"Yes, we shall."

"Have you been to Casino d'Ambre?"

"No, and I really, really need to see that." She gave him a big smile and held out her hand. "Let's get out of here."

Half an hour later, as he took Lucy on a tour of Montedoro's world-famous casino, Damien was feeling more than a little guilty about his behavior at the villa. He'd been gruff with her when he'd had no reason to be—other than he'd been kissing her and touching her and thoroughly enjoying himself. And then the phone had gone off twice and ruined the moment.

He'd felt rotten—about V and her games. About Lucy witnessing once again what a bad choice he'd made in getting involved with V in the first place. About how his life seemed somehow rudderless lately, without direction.

Which was absurd, really. He'd always taken life as it came and had a fine time of it. He was *still* having a fine time of it, and he didn't plan to change.

Lucy took it all in stride. She didn't let his earlier bad attitude put a damper on the day. She didn't push; she didn't sulk. She was as lighthearted and full of fun as ever, wide-eyed at the beauty of the legendary casino, clapping when some tourist won a bundle at roulette.

After the Casino d'Ambre, they strolled the shops of the Triangle d'Or, the area of exclusive stores, restaurants and hotels surrounding the casino square. Workers were everywhere that day putting up the Christmas decorations around the square, ushering in the season. Holiday music filled the air.

Damien took Lucy's hand as they walked. He leaned close and teasingly reminded her to pay no attention to the ever-present paparazzi. He made an effort to be extra attentive after the uncomfortable moments at the villa.

They'd stopped to watch a couple of burly workmen hang a giant lit wreath above a shop door when she sighed and sent him one of her dewy-eyed smiles. "Christmas in Montedoro. I'll bet it's almost as beautiful as Christmas in Manhattan."

He squeezed her fingers, twined with his. "I know your brother is angling to get you to go home to California."

"He can angle all he wants. I'll be in New York City for the holiday season. Just wait and see."

He let go of her hand so he could wrap an arm around her and pull her closer. She laughed, a happy, carefree sound. And so he bent his head and kissed her, right there on the Triangle d'Or for the two workmen and the crowds of busy shoppers and everyone else to see.

When they started walking again, he kept his arm around her and she leaned her head on his shoulder. "Thank you, Dami. For giving me this beautiful, perfect Thanksgiving. It's turning out to be everything I could have hoped for."

He pressed his lips to her fragrant hair. "No thanks are needed. Ever. You know that."

She looked up at him then. Her eyes were so solemn. "You are the most generous person I know."

He wasn't, and she really ought to remember that. "Not really."

She elbowed him in the ribs. "Yeah. Really."

"If you keep making me sound so exemplary, I'll decide it wouldn't be right to seduce you this evening."

She widened her eyes in pretended terror. "Omigod, no! I take it all back. You're a horrible man, a scoundrel, a total dog."

He flattened his lips and arched an eyebrow, going for an evil leer. "Wonderful. You've convinced me. I'll be taking complete advantage of you after all."

They returned to the palace a short time later. By then it was a little after six. There was a light buffet laid out on a sideboard in the main dining room. They filled plates and sat together to eat.

After that he walked her to her room. He kissed her, a kiss he let go on a little too long. A kiss that tempted him to push the door open behind her, to carry her in there and finish what they'd started the night before.

But no. Once he had her naked in his arms, he wasn't going to want to let her go until the morning, when they would say goodbye. And tonight was the annual Prince's Thanksgiving Ball. She couldn't miss that. It was a memorable part of a Montedoran Thanksgiving.

Reluctantly, he broke the kiss and promised to return for her at nine.

In his apartment, Damien got out his phone, turned on the ringer again and checked his messages and calls. He discovered that V had called only those two times. And left one voice mail.

He sat for a while actually considering calling her, trying one more time to speak reasonably with her, to convince her that she had to leave it alone, move on. And then he went ahead and played back her message even though he never played her messages anymore, because he'd grown weary of listening to her call him bad names in Italian.

Surprisingly, her voice was calm. She spoke English, which surprised him almost as much as her even tone. V was fluent in English, but she considered it a barbaric language, unmusical and crass.

"Dami. I can guess where you are. With that skinny, plain little American nobody, the one with hardly any hair." A laugh, soft, knowing. The bitch. "You're all over the internet with her, the two of you at the bazaar on Thursday and the museum last night. Really, Dami, what am I going to do with you?" A long sigh. "I know, I know. You have to follow every cheap flirtation to its logical conclusion and I'm going to have to leave you alone to pursue this new and incomprehensible infatuation. And guess what—I believe I will do just that. Enjoy yourself. I've had enough. When you finally see what a fool you've been, you'll be sorry. But of course, there won't be anything you can do about it. Because I am finished. You hear me? It's over, *finito. Ciao.*"

Damien got up from the sofa and paced to the window. He wasn't angry, exactly, just annoyed at her spiteful remarks about Lucy, who never hurt anyone, who only brought joy.

And there was a bright side to this. Or there could be. V had sounded as though she'd finally accepted the inevitable.

He put the phone to his ear again and played the message through a second time.

Yes. Very possibly a real goodbye.

He went back to the sofa, kicked off his shoes and stretched out. A certain buoyancy had come over him. He felt distinctly optimistic.

It didn't hurt his new, improved mood that for now,

anyway, there was no need to consider calling V after all. If she'd meant what she'd said, he wouldn't be talking to her again.

And if she hadn't meant it...

Well, he'd walk that plank when he came to it.

"I work as a nanny," said Lani Vasquez, leaning closer to Lucy in order to be heard over the din in the crowded ballroom. The musicians had taken a break and now everyone seemed to be talking at once. Lani went on, "I came from Texas with Sydney when she married Rule." *Rule,* Lucy reminded herself. *Second-born after Maximilian.* "And now I take care of their kids, Trevor and Ellie. It's such a great job. I love the kids and Sydney is very hands-on, so I get a lot of time to myself. Tonight she and Rule are at their villa with the children, so here I am enjoying the Thanksgiving Ball." Lani flashed a bright smile. "I love it here in Montedoro. I never want to leave."

Prince Maximilian, the heir apparent, who'd been standing a few feet away chatting with a beefy older guy, stepped closer. He and the black-haired nanny from Texas shared a warm glance. "Lani's a writer," he said. "She's writing a series of historical novels set in Montedoro."

"Someday I intend to be a *published* writer," Lani added. "Someday *soon,* I keep hoping."

"Lani has an agent in America," said the prince. The man was clearly a booster of the pretty nanny. "She's right on the brink of that first big sale."

"The brink." Lani gave a small uncomfortable chuckle. "As I said, we can hope."

"It can't be long now." Max seemed to have no doubts about Lani's inevitable success.

"His Highness has two children, Nicholas and Constance," Lani told Lucy.

"I remember seeing them at Thanksgiving dinner." Lucy pictured them: a dark-eyed boy of seven or eight, a little blonde girl a year or two younger.

Lani went on, "Their nanny, Gerta, and I have become good friends."

Max said, "Gerta's like a second mother to them. They're very attached to her."

"Gerta. I've heard that name before— Wait, I know. Dami told me that he had a nanny named Gerta."

"That's right," Max replied. "Gerta was our nanny, too. She looked after all nine of us when we were small. Gerta's part of the family, really."

Lani said, "We all hang out together. The four children, Gerta and I. That's how Max and I have gotten to know each other a little. His Highness is the world's foremost expert on the history of Montedoro." She said it proudly, with real admiration, apparently as much a booster of the prince as he was of her. "And he's arranged it so that I have unlimited access to the amazing original materials in the palace library."

"Wow." Lucy was impressed. "Talk about an invaluable research resource...."

Lani and the prince shared another lingering glance. "Exactly," Lani said. "The library contains the correspondence of the Calabretti princes over hundreds of years. There are historical documents going back to the Middle Ages. I could never find such a treasure trove anywhere else."

Right then Dami, who'd gone off to chat up some business associate, appeared at Lucy's side. He greeted his brother and Lani. The music began to play again.

Max offered Lani his hand. She took it and they went out on the floor to dance.

Lucy watched them go. "The prince and the nanny. I'm lovin' it."

"What are you talking about?" Dami sounded surprised.

Lucy chuckled. "Oh, come on." She watched the two dancing. They had eyes only for each other. "It's obvious those two have a thing going on."

"No. Never." His tone was flat, unequivocal. She glanced at him. He was frowning. And then he said grudgingly, "Yes, all right. It's a little odd."

"Excuse me? Odd?"

"Max only dances with his sisters and our mother."

"Well, yeah. That is kind of odd."

"That's not what I meant. You don't understand." He watched Max and Lani until they danced out of sight. Then he shook his head. "Never mind."

She moved in a fraction closer to him and brushed her bare arm against the superfine wool of his sleeve, loving the heat in her belly, the shiver of anticipation for the night to come, when it would be just the two of them at last and they would finally finish what they'd started the night before. "Don't blow me off, Dami. There's something going on between the two of them. They're a mutual admiration society, I kid you not. And when they look at each other... Bam." She lifted her fisted hands and then popped all her fingers wide to illustrate.

Dami eased an arm around her waist and drew her in front of him. She felt him at her back and longed to lean into his heat and hardness. However, if she did that, she'd probably start rubbing on him next. And it wouldn't be appropriate to go all X-rated at the Prince's Thanksgiving Ball.

He said in her ear, "Max loved his wife, Sophia. He loved her and only her from the time they were children. When he lost her, we all worried that he wouldn't be able to go on."

She craned her head back to him. He dipped his closer. She said, "And that's all so romantic, I know. But hey. The guy's still alive. He has a right to a little happiness with someone who's still breathing, don't you think?"

"Luce." He spoke into her ear again and his warm breath stirred her hair. "I'm only telling you that you've got it all wrong."

She craned her head back once more. "No. Sorry. You're the one who doesn't get it. I know what I saw."

He caught her hand. Heat shimmered up her arm from the point of contact as he whirled her to face him. His dark eyes glittered, inviting her. "Dance with me."

She became sharply aware once again that she had no panties on. Her belly hollowed out and her breath caught. And she felt very naughty and wonderful and wild. "I was wondering if you were ever going to ask."

He pulled her out on the floor and took her in his arms.

Dancing with Dami. It was as easy and natural as breathing, though Lucy had never been that good of a dancer. She hadn't had a whole lot of opportunities to practice. Dami, on the other hand, was a *great* dancer. He could make any woman look good on the dance floor.

He had danced with her on the night that she'd met him. Noah had thrown one of his parties that night. There'd been a six-piece combo and dancing outside on the loggia. Prince Damien had asked her to dance and she'd felt like a princess. A very skinny, rather pale princess, it was true. At the time, she'd still been recovering from that final surgery. But that night, being too skinny with dark circles under her eyes didn't matter. She'd felt like a princess dancing with Dami, knowing already that he would be her friend.

Now he held her so lightly, guided her so effortlessly. Her gown, strapless navy-and-black organza and guipure, seemed to float around her peep-toe high heels, unhampered by boring gravity. They danced two dances.

And then Noah cut in. "Mind if I dance with my beautiful sister?"

With a graceful nod, Dami surrendered her to her brother.

She went into Noah's arms and watched Dami's broad back as he wove his way through the other dancers, moving toward the full bar set up between a pair of marble pillars in a far corner.

"Your dress is beautiful," Noah said. She thanked him. "What time's your flight tomorrow?"

She suppressed a sigh. After all, she'd told him more than once before. "Eleven-thirty."

"We haven't seen enough of you over the weekend."

"I know, it was a short visit. But I've had a wonderful time."

A hesitation, then, "With Damien."

She returned his gaze, unwavering. "Yes, Noah. With Damien."

They danced for several seconds without speaking, which was fine with her. Then he said, "Dami's a good man."

"He's the best."

"If he hurts you, I might have to kill him."

"Oh, stop it. Dami would never hurt me. And no matter what happens, you don't get to kill him. Murder is a bad thing— Plus, Alice would never forgive you if you killed her brother."

He scowled. "You've become so…stubborn and determined the past few years."

"I was always stubborn and determined, but when I was sick all the time, I didn't have the energy to be my real self."

After a moment, he slanted her a sideways look. "How about Christmas?"

She couldn't help laughing. "Do you ever give up?"

A wry smile curved his lips. "Never. I'm a lot like my baby sister that way."

"Noah, I'm serious. I keep thinking we're clear that I run my own life at last. And then you come at me again."

He did look contrite. "Sorry."

"Are you really?"

He nodded. "I get that you're feeling good, doing what you want to do and loving every minute of it. And that's great. I just… I still want to protect you. I can't turn that off overnight."

"Keep working on it, will you?"

"I am, Lucy. Honestly."

"Work faster, then." She said it gently. With all the love in her heart. "Please."

Lani Vasquez and Prince Maximilian whirled by them, eyes only for each other. And Lucy thought of Dami's surprise and disbelief when she'd said that there was something going on between them. Was it always like that in families? People got locked into roles—the sickly one, the grieving widower—and other family members just refused to see that the ones they love can change and grow.

But then Noah said, "Just remember that I'm proud of you. You were right to strike out on your own, not to let my fears for you hold you back. I wish you were coming home for the holidays, but if you insist on staying in New York, I'll get over it. Have a beautiful Christmas, Lucy."

So, then. Maybe her brother's view of her wasn't so locked in after all. She wished him the best Christmas ever and when that dance ended, he walked her over to the bar, where Dami and Alice were sipping champagne.

Alice set down her glass and held out her hand to Noah. He led her out on the floor. They gazed at each other the same way Prince Max had looked at Lani Vasquez.

Dami handed Lucy a crystal flute of champagne. They raised their glasses to the season. And when their glasses were empty, he asked her to dance again. It was an old standard that time, a slow holiday song: "What Are You Doing New Year's Eve?"

She felt a little sad to think that on New Year's Eve she would be in New York and Dami would be somewhere else. But not *that* sad.

Really, how could she be sad? She was getting exactly what she'd dreamed of: a fabulous Thanksgiving weekend and tender lessons in lovemaking from a man she trusted absolutely.

When that dance was over, she whispered, "It's long past midnight. I don't want to wait anymore, Dami."

He gave her a look that was totally hot. And then he took her hand and led her out of the crowded ballroom.

Chapter Eight

His sheets were gold that night. Gold satin.

They stood beside the beautiful carved bed with the finials shaped like crowns, the gold sheets turned back, lustrous and inviting in the soft low light. He kissed her for the longest time, an endless, tender, ever-deepening kiss.

As he kissed her, he touched her, caressing her bare shoulders, her back, the curve of her waist and lower. When he stroked his hands over her hips, she moaned a little, sharply aware of her nakedness beneath the long skirt of her dress.

Really, a woman's panties didn't cover all that much to make her feel so bare without them. But she did feel bare under her gown. Bare and revealed, somehow, though no one could see.

He lifted his mouth from hers. "Luce."

"Um?"

"Take off your dress."

"Yes." She turned around and showed him her back. He pulled her zipper down. The dress fell away. She caught it, stepped out of it, tossed it toward the nearest chair.

"No panties," he said approvingly.

She turned to face him. "I'm very obedient. When I want to be."

His eyes burned into hers. "The rest. Take it off."

So she did. Everything. There wasn't that much. Her strapless bra. Her peep-toe shoes. Her vintage earrings and antique bracelet.

He took the jewelry from her, set it on the table by the bed. And then, still fully clothed except for the jacket he'd taken off when they first entered the apartment, he started touching her again. He bent and kissed her breasts as his hands went roaming.

Time fell away and her knees went all wobbly. But Dami didn't let her fall. He scooped her up against his broad chest and then sat on the edge of the bed with her in his lap.

His skilled, knowing hands moved over her. She looked down at his long fingers against the pale flesh of her belly. Those fingers stroked lower.

And lower. He parted her. She didn't have to be told. She eased her thighs apart.

"Wider," he whispered, the word hot and a little bit rough. He scraped the side of her throat with his teeth.

She moaned. And she obeyed. It was only what she wanted after all. His fingers found her, delving in, moving in a rhythm her body already knew and welcomed.

"Dami," she cried. "Yes…more…" She tipped her head back and gave him her mouth for a slow, wet, hungry kiss.

He whispered things, naughty things. Each whisper took her higher, closer to the sky, to the darkness and the wonder.

To that moment when it all burst wide open into a midnight universe scattered with a million exploding stars.

It happened so quickly: her body contracting, pulsing, a fast, hard, beautiful climax. And then he was lifting her, laying her down across the gold sheets, pushing her thighs wide again as he knelt on the rug by the bed.

She felt his breath first, there, at the core of her. Then the skilled, tender stroking of his tongue.

And then, just like that, she was going over again, falling from one peak into the next one. Rising, rising and shattering again, stronger, deeper, better than the first time, as she clutched his dark head and moaned how she wanted him, how right it was, how perfect, exactly what she'd been dreaming of.

When he pulled away and stood over her, she didn't have the strength to hold him. She let out a little moan of satisfaction, a sigh of pleasured fulfillment. Still crosswise on the bed, her legs limp and dangling over the side, she closed her eyes and drifted on a sea of delicious afterglow.

Until he touched her again, the lightest brush of a touch, one finger tracking down from her hip bone to her thigh, to her knee, along her shin....

"Dami?" She opened her eyes to find him naked and so very fine, all broad, hard, muscled manliness, kneeling on the rug again. "Dami..." She reached for him.

He rose and leaned over her, bending close and kissing her, a quick, hard kiss. And then he lifted her, rearranging her so that she was full-length on the bed with her head on the pillows. He stretched out beside her.

She buried her face against his chest, breathed in his scent of sea foam and musk and man.

And the wonder began all over again. He kissed her—arousing, hungry, lingering kisses. First on her lips and then along her throat, across her chest, her breasts, her belly. He opened his mouth on her, using his tongue and, so carefully and deliberately, his strong white teeth.

By then she was wild for him, tossing her head on the pillows, begging him, "Please, Dami, please," as she clutched him with her hungry hands, pulling at him, yearning for the moment when she would have him within her.

He took his time about that. He drove her up to the brink again with his hands and his hot mouth—and then, just when she knew she was going over a third time that night without him inside her, he lifted up and eased his hard, hair-rough thigh between her two soft ones.

She opened her eyes and he was above her, gazing down at her, his eyes so dark, edged in deepest green.

He put one hand on either of her thighs and pushed them wide. She knew he could see everything. And that only made her hotter, made her want him more.

"Dami." She was breathless. So hungry. Needing. Wanting. Everything. All of him, now. "Please..."

"Now, Luce?"

She looked down between them and saw that he was more than ready for her. And also that somehow he had already put on the protection she'd totally forgotten they were going to need.

"Luce." He growled her name.

And she looked in his face again. "Um. I..."

"Now?" Softly that time. Patiently. Tenderly, too.

"Um, yes. Yes. Please. Now…."

He braced his forearms to either side of her, cradling her head between his two hands. "Look at me."

She nodded, eager. A little bit scared, too, thinking again of the size of him.

Would there be pain? How much?

"Stay with me." His eyes were on her. She met them, held them.

And then she felt him, nudging her where she was so wet and soft and sensitive now. The tip slid in. Wonderful. Perfect.

"More," she said on a low moan.

He gave her exactly what she asked for, sliding in by slow degrees.

It was good. It was heaven.

And then it was too much. And then it was hurting. She gasped, "Oh! I… Wait."

"Shh," he said. "It's all right." He lowered his head, pressed his forehead to hers. "We'll wait…."

They lay there half joined, still. Waiting. Her breath came swift and hungry; her body felt stretched, aching.

And then the ache was changing, easing into something electric and wonderful again.

She lifted her head and kissed his mouth, whispering, "Yes. Now," against his parted lips.

"More?" It came out on a low groan.

She nodded. "More…"

And he went deeper—until she gasped again.

Instantly, he went still for her. There was only the sound of their breathing, the burning down low that once again eased and changed to a thrilling fullness.

She said it again. "More…"

He bent his head, captured her breast, drew on it in slow, deep pulls.

That did it. She moaned and clutched him close to her, lifting to meet him that time as he went deeper.

And deeper.

And then, with a low, hard groan, he was in all the way, filling her completely.

Finally. At last.

She laughed a little, then stopped on a moan. "Oh, Dami. Yes."

He was still again, waiting for her untried body to accept his invasion.

"Yes," she said, pushing against him.

"Sure?" It came out a rough, painful growl.

"Yes. Yes, yes, yes..."

And then, at last, he started to move.

He did it carefully at first, gently, with slow deliberation. Bracing up his hands to give himself better control, he kept his thrusts steady, even.

But she was more than ready by then, more than eager. She lifted her hands and clasped his big shoulders and held on good and tight as she moved in rhythm with him.

She tried to keep her eyes open to see his face above her, to imprint every burning, beautiful second of this wonder into her memory, to seal it in her heart.

But the pleasure was too overwhelming. It was raising her up, making her dizzy with the flood of sensation. There was nothing to do in the end but surrender to it.

She closed her eyes. And once again she was whirling up and up—and over the edge of the world into an explosion of light and sensation as she felt her body pulsing around him, felt him surge into her deeper, fuller, harder even than before.

And by then she could only hold on and keep sighing,

"Yes, yes, yes," as the pulsing faded down to a lovely glow of happy satisfaction.

At seven o'clock on Sunday morning, Dami gave her a robe to wear and led her to the kitchen, where he made her coffee and served her croissants from Justine's café. She ate two. They were so good and she was hungry.

Then she returned to his bedroom and put on her clothes from the night before as he stood in the doorway, big arms across his broad chest, watching her, his expression unreadable.

Yeah, it was a little sad. A little strange. To be leaving him so soon after the complete fabulousness of last night.

But she remembered what she'd promised herself at his studio. Not to cling. Not to linger. She scooped up her evening clutch and went to him with a bright smile.

At the door to the outer hall, she kissed him. His mouth touched hers, tasting of coffee, making her long to lift her arms and pull him closer. It was early yet. They had time.

To share more kisses. To make love again in the morning light.

But no. That would only hurt more in the end. She was on her way now. Better to keep moving, go back to her room, get her things packed, call a cab....

She kept her arms at her sides and when he lifted his head, she said, "It was perfect, Dami."

He framed her face between his hands and there was such an ache within her. The end had come way too soon. Already she missed the beauty and rightness of all they had shared. "Travel safe, Luce."

She pressed her lips to his once more. "Have the best Christmas ever."

"You, too." His hands fell away.

She turned from him.

He reached around her and pushed open the door for her. She went out into the wide, beautiful hallway and started walking.

She didn't glance back to find out if he watched her leaving him. She didn't need the temptation of seeing him there staring after her—or worse, *not* seeing him.

Better not to look. Better not to know.

Chapter Nine

"Lucy, wait up!"

Her arms full of groceries, Lucy backed against the entry door, holding it open as Brandon Delaney jogged up the building steps toward her, wearing heavy running pants, a winter-weight hoodie and cross-trainers, his cap on backward.

Once he cleared the door, she let it swing shut. He was panting pretty hard, his handsome face red, his blond hair sweaty where it stuck out from under the cap.

"When did you get back?" he asked between breaths.

"Sunday."

"Good trip?"

"It was terrific, thanks." She flashed him a smile, wondering how he knew she'd been gone. She hadn't told him she was going away for Thanksgiving. Maybe Ed, the super, had mentioned her trip, or Viviana Nichols, who lived in the larger apartment on her floor, might have said something to him.

Flashing her a broad smile that showed off a dental hygienist's dream of straight, brilliantly white teeth, Brandon reached for her groceries. "Here. Let me carry those for you."

Okay. Weird. Brandon had been avoiding her for a couple of weeks, ever since she'd put that pitiful excuse for a move on him. Why was he suddenly so friendly now?

Then again, what did it matter why he was being nice? If he wanted to carry her stuff, wonderful.

The elevator had stopped up on five. Rather than wait for it, they took the stairs. Lucy's apartment was on the third floor. As they trudged up the two flights, he said, "I had no idea that you knew the prince."

He knew she knew Dami? She was certain she'd never told him that.

On second thought, it probably wasn't such a stretch that he would know. Pictures of her and Dami were not only all over the internet but they had made a few of the tabloids, too. Brandon could have seen them. "Yes. We're good friends."

"Wow." He shook his head. "Amazing. Thanksgiving at the Prince's Palace. That must have been something."

"How did you know I was in Montedoro?"

"Marie. She had a copy of the *National Enquirer*. She showed me the pictures of you and the prince. You know how she is...."

Marie Dobronsky, the super's wife, was a sweet woman. She did like to gossip, however. Lucy made a mental note not to be so chatty with Marie in the future.

They reached the second floor and started up to the third. Brandon said, "I don't think I've ever seen him here— I mean, I heard that he does own the building. Is that right?"

"Yes, he does," she said, and left it at that. They reached her floor. Brandon fell in behind her as she approached her door. "Thanks. You can just set the bags down. I'll take it from here."

"Oh, come on. Let me carry them in for you."

She started to refuse—but wait a minute. A week ago she would have been walking on air to have Brandon carrying her groceries for her. "Hey, if you insist…" She unlocked the door and ushered him in first, pointing down the short hall that opened into her small living room and the kitchen beyond. "That way."

He carried the bags in and set them on the retro chrome-and-red laminate table she'd found on eBay. "This is nice." He took off his cap and looked around her tiny narrow kitchen, which had a small skinny window with a view of a brick wall. Her cat, Boris, sat in that window, watching them with a bored expression on his broad face. Brandon turned his blinding white smile her way again. "We should catch up. Let's go get coffee or something."

Coffee. He wanted to get a coffee with her….

Last Wednesday she would have traded her Juki serger sewing machine for a chance to get a coffee with Brandon. But after Dami, well, Brandon somehow wasn't giving her the familiar thrill.

And that totally annoyed her.

The whole point of convincing Dami to teach her about sex had been to become more experienced, more sophisticated—not to lose all interest in Brandon, who was a good part of the reason she'd asked for Dami's help in the first place.

Uh-uh. No way was she turning down a coffee with

Brandon. Even if she didn't want to go. "How about the diner on the corner? But I need to put this food away first."

"I'll grab a shower, be back for you in twenty."

Lucy loved the Paradise Diner. It was owned by a Greek family, the Mustos, and served the usual diner fare, burgers and fries, meat loaf and mashed potatoes, coffee and pie—plus a few Greek specialties. The cook, Nestor, was a little scary. Sometimes he shouted through the service window in Greek. The waitresses treated Lucy like one of the family. There was just something so homey and comfortable about the Paradise. Lucy ate there every chance she got.

While she'd been out of town, they'd decorated for the holidays, painting the windows with Christmas greetings, hanging fat gold garland everywhere, putting up an artificial tree by the cash register and an almost-life-size crèche in the corner by the door.

She and Brandon took a booth and ordered coffee and pie. Brandon talked about the auditions he'd been on and the part he thought he was sure to get in an upcoming off-Broadway show. And his agent was pushing him to fly out to L.A. and audition for a major role in a new sitcom. Yeah, it was just television. But a guy had to eat.

And then he leaned closer. "Come on, Lucy. Are you sure you and Prince Damien aren't having a *thing?*"

She laughed at that. "Like I said, we're just friends." It caused a distinct ache in her heart to say those words. Maybe more of an ache than she'd bargained for. "He's always been good to me, that's all."

"'Good to you.'" Brandon arched a golden eyebrow. "I could take that any number of ways."

What was that supposed to mean? She didn't even want to know. "Why should you take it *any* way? Sheesh, Brandon. Are you writing a book or something?"

He gave her that blinding white smile again, the one that just a couple of weeks ago could rock her world. "I'm an actor. It's my job to understand what makes people tick—and 'always'? You said he's 'always' been good to you. Does that mean you've known him since childhood?"

Pushy. There was no other word for the way Brandon was behaving. And in any case, she just didn't feel comfortable discussing Dami with a casual acquaintance. Privacy mattered to Dami, to all the Bravo-Calabrettis. She doubted Brandon would go running to the tabloids with something she said. But still.

She said, "He's a friend of the family."

Brandon wouldn't quit. "I saw somewhere, I think, that your brother is marrying his sister Princess Alice."

"Yes," she answered with zero inflection. "They're very happy together."

He gave her a sly look from those golden-brown eyes she used to drool over. "Lucy, you are turning out to be a very big surprise."

And that had her feeling defensive somehow. "I'm the same person I was before."

"Well, yeah. But I just didn't know…" He was looking at her so intently, his gaze tracking from her eyes to her mouth and back to her eyes again. "God. Was I blind or what?"

Flirting. Omigod. Brandon Delaney was flirting with her. He was flirting with her and she didn't even care. In fact, it was kind of depressing that he was interested now and she felt nothing but vaguely annoyed with him. "Brandon, eat your pie."

He went on looking at her in that teasingly intimate way. "I want to spend more time with you."

She couldn't resist reminding him, "But I'm so innocent, remember? And you've got no time for me, because acting is your life."

He leaned his chin on his fist and gave her the long, lingering, melting, butterscotch stare. "I've changed my mind."

Yeah, well. So had she. She opened her mouth to tell him so—and his phone, which he'd set on the table beside him, started playing "Gangnam Style."

He snatched it up and looked at the screen. "I need to take this." And he did. Right then and there. "Maureen... Yes...They do?...Yes!" He flashed Lucy a thumbs-up. She had no idea why. "Tomorrow? Impossible...." He scowled. She could hear the person named Maureen talking fast. And Brandon started nodding. "Yeah, I do. I know...You're right, okay, tomorrow." There was more. He kept on agreeing with the person named Maureen and said that yes, he would, absolutely. He was on it. Lucy finished her excellent pie and sipped her coffee.

When he finally hung up, she guessed, "Big news?"

"Oh, yeah. That was my agent. That sitcom I told you about? They want me. They *really* want me. I'm flying out to L.A. tonight. It's big, Lucy. It's huge—and listen, I've got to get moving...."

"Absolutely." She wished him good luck in theater speak. "Break a leg."

He was already on his feet. "Thanks, Lucy."

"Break them both."

He chuckled. Then he bent close and kissed her on the cheek. "We'll talk...soon."

"'Bye, Brandon."

He straightened, turned and headed for the door.

Lucy watched him go. He hadn't touched his pie.

The waitress, Tabitha, who was the owner's daughter and around Lucy's age, appeared beside the booth, coffeepot in hand. She refilled Lucy's cup. "Not your type, huh?"

Lucy reached across the table and snagged Brandon's abandoned pie. "Was I that obvious?"

"Not to him, apparently—and look. He left you something." She waved the check.

Laughing, Lucy took it. "Not a problem. After all, I get to eat his pie."

It snowed the next day, Thursday. Not a lot. But enough that Lucy could look out her bedroom windows and see it drifting down onto the sidewalk outside, a frail bit of it collecting in the dip of the brown awning over the door of the Italian restaurant across the street. She wished Dami was there to see it with her.

And then she felt gloomy. Because he wasn't there, because it was only a little snow and she still wanted to share it with him.

She couldn't stop thinking about him. And she tried to excuse that by telling herself it was natural to miss him after all that had happened between them. It wasn't that bad to have maybe fallen for him just a little bit— not too much, oh, no. Only a thoroughly appropriate amount given that he'd seen her naked more than once and she'd done things with him she'd never done in her life before.

Good things. Wonderful things. Things she couldn't let herself think too much about or she'd only get gloomier.

Keeping busy. That was the key. No way was she

going to end up sitting in a chair staring out the window, thinking of Thanksgiving and wanting to cry.

As soon as the snow stopped, she went out and prowled her favorite fabric and notions stores, snatching up things that inspired her. She intended to work for several hours every day on clothing and accessory designs and on making a few of the ideas she came up with.

Lots of work should keep her from longing for Dami.

And, hey, it was Christmastime. There were so many organizations looking for volunteers.

On Friday morning she looked around online and chose two worthy causes. She called and signed up to wrap presents for disadvantaged kids and to put in five four-hour sessions making costumes for a children's theater organization called Make-Believe and Magic. She worked for a while sketching a few new accessory designs and then she went down the street to the Paradise for a late breakfast.

By then the regular breakfast crowd had cleared out and the diner was quiet for that hour or two before they all started piling in for lunch.

Tabby gave her coffee, took her order, stuck it on the rack in the pass-through for Nestor and then slid into the seat across from her. "Wow, Lucy. You always look so great."

"Thanks." Lucy fluffed the cowl neck of the white sweater she wore under her cutaway purple jacket. "Clothes are my undying passion, it's true."

"Didn't you say once that you make everything you wear?"

"Most of them, I do." She picked up her coffee cup.

Tabby was looking at her kind of strangely. "Okay." She sipped. "Something's on your mind. What?"

"God. I don't even know how to ask you...."

"Oh, come on. I'm totally harmless. Ask me."

Tabby puffed out her cheeks with a hard breath. "There's this guy. I've had my eye on him. He finally asked me out for Saturday, a week from tomorrow night. It's a cocktail-dress thing—and I mean, I know it's really short notice, but then I was thinking how you have such amazing taste and all and maybe you could give me a few tips on what to buy, that you could—"

"You want me to make something for you? I could so do that."

Tabby blinked. "Just like that. You would—you *could?*"

"Yeah. It would be fun."

"I would pay you. I mean, not a lot, but—"

Lucy waved a hand. "Not a problem. I'm just getting started in my career, anyway. I need cool projects."

"But I *would* pay you."

"Sure. Of course. We can work that out."

"But...I mean, something for *me,* right? For my body and coloring? Your style is killer, but it's not me." Tabby had streaky blond hair and amazing cheekbones. She stood five-eleven or so and rocked one of those real-woman bodies with serious curves.

"Oh, yeah. For you, only you. I'm thinking something that flows and clings and shows off a little of that gorgeous olive skin."

Tabitha asked in a breathless tone, "Can it be red?"

"Oh, yes, it can."

All at once Tabby looked like a kid having the best Christmas ever. "Lucy, I'm liking this. I seriously am...."

* * *

Tabby came right over to Lucy's after her shift was through.

Lucy ushered her into the bedroom, which was big enough that she not only had her bed and dresser in there but she'd also set up a cutting table, her two sewing machines and a couple of dress forms. Lucy took Tabby's measurements and they discussed fabric and detail. Lucy was thinking the red dress should be chiffon, with a flowing short skirt, a ruched strapless bodice and a sweetheart neckline. And there should be bling— maybe crystal beading or rhinestones to accent the bodice. She did some quick sketches and Tabby was sold. She wrote a check right then and there for the amount Lucy quoted her.

Then they started talking. Tabby talked about the guy who'd asked her out for Saturday night. His name was Henry O'Mara and he owned a shoe-repair shop in Chelsea. She said her parents were driving her crazy. She'd been engaged to a nice Greek man, but she'd called it off and they couldn't understand what could be the matter with her. Lucy shared her issues with Noah and her adoration of Alice. She even talked about Dami a little.

Tabby said, "Leave it to you to find yourself a prince."

And Lucy said the usual, "It's not like that. We're just friends."

At which Tabby made a snorting sound. "Yeah. Right. Like I believe that."

They ended up going across the street to the Italian place, where they each ordered the sausage ravioli. When they got back to Lucy's, Viviana Nichols opened her door. She had a plate of cookies fresh from the oven and she grinned at them, the lines around her eyes deepening, her brown face full of fun and mischief. So they joined her in her warm, cookie-scented kitchen for coffee and snicker doodles.

Later that night, alone in her apartment, Lucy felt pretty good about everything. She loved New York, she couldn't wait for her first semester at FIT NY and she had a feeling Tabby was going to be a real friend.

Okay, yes, she did miss Dami a lot. It had been nearly a week since she'd left him. She wanted to call him. But that somehow felt wrong. She'd been the one who'd initiated their weekend together, and she'd done it with the clear understanding that they would both walk away in the end. She'd promised herself she wouldn't pester him, which meant she needed to leave him alone for a while, till after the holidays, at least. And she absolutely would *not* be disappointed that he hadn't gotten in touch.

In the early half of the following week, Brandon called to tell her that he now had "several potential projects" lined up and would be staying in Los Angeles until after the New Year.

"And, Lucy…" His voice trailed off. He let out a long sigh. "I really like you, but I've met someone. Someone special. I may end up subletting my apartment and staying on here indefinitely. But in any case, it looks like it won't be happening for you and me after all."

Lucy told him she was happy for him and wished him well. She hung up with a feeling of relief that Brandon Delaney had found love in L.A. and that private "talk" he'd said he wanted to have with her would never be happening.

The next day, her brother called to see if maybe she'd changed her mind about coming home for Christmas. She told him—again—that she hadn't. He put Alice on and they discussed *the* dress. A little while later Hannah called just to chat.

Every time her phone rang, she couldn't quell a little thrill of hope that it might be Dami.

But it never was.

She bought gifts for her family, got them wrapped and packed and sent them off. She put in some hours making costumes for the Make-Believe and Magic Children's Theatre Company. And she made Tabby's red cocktail dress. Tabby came over Thursday for a final fitting. "Wow," she said, twirling in front of Lucy's full-length mirror. "Is that really me?"

"It's you and you are spectacular. Now stand up straight. That's it." Lucy marked the hem. "It'll be ready tomorrow. You can pick it up after your shift at the diner."

They went over to the Italian place to grab a bite to eat and Tabby insisted on paying the check. "You made me look fabulous. I can at least buy dinner."

Friday morning Lucy hemmed Tabby's dress and gave it a finishing press. She had lunch with Viviana, who made them turkey-pesto paninis and black-eyed-pea soup and then hardly touched either.

"Missin' my Joseph today," Viv said softly in that husky voice of hers, her beautiful dark eyes full of shadows. Her husband had died eighteen years ago in December. She and Joseph had owned two dry-cleaning stores, long since sold. "Missin' my babies, too." She had two daughters and six grandchildren. Two of the grandchildren were older than Lucy. Her eyes brightened a little. "I'll be going to Shoshona's for Christmas…." Shoshona was the older daughter. She lived in Chicago. Marleah lived in Denver. "You should go home for the holiday, sweet girl. Be with your family. We all need family at Christmas."

Lucy could not deny she felt a little ache in her heart right then to go home to the big house in Carpinteria that Hannah would have all done up for the holidays, to be with them—Alice and Hannah and even her bossy big brother. She longed suddenly to ride Dammerlicht, a steady-natured, smart Hanoverian, her favorite in her brother's fine stable of beautiful horses. She yearned to watch the sun set over the Pacific.

But no. She'd made her decision and she was sticking with it. "I'm spending my holiday right here in Manhattan, Viv. It's my first year on my own."

Viviana waved a heavily veined, beautifully manicured hand. "Pah. I've been on my own for almost twenty years now. My girls keep after me to move near one of them. They think I'm too old to be taking care of myself. But this is home. I love New York and I'm an independent soul. I keep busy and I'm happy with my life. But for Christmas, being alone sucks."

An hour later, Viv gave her a plateful of sugar cookies and she returned to her apartment.

She got out one of her sketchbooks and sat in the corner chair in her bedroom. With the plate of cookies in reach, she got to work on some ideas she had for Alice's wedding dress, which was to be totally Alice: dramatic and daring, with a very low back framed in lace, snugly fitted past the hips, flaring out to an ocean of lace and tulle.

An hour flew by. She sketched and munched cookies and the dress took shape. And then the buzzer downstairs rang. It was Tabby, running over on her break to pick up her dress. Lucy gave it to her, along with a couple of cookies. They chatted for a few minutes. Tabby grabbed her in a hug and was gone.

Lucy went back to work. About a half an hour later she glanced up and saw the moving haze of white out the window.

Snow.

Real snow this time, the flakes so thick and white, like a moving veil softly obscuring the buildings across the street. Perfect. Beautiful. Her first snowy Christmastime in all of her life.

If only Dami...

She cut off the thought. He wasn't there. He wouldn't *be* there. And she was going to be absolutely fine with that. She had a good life, damn it. A life that she'd fought for, a life in an exciting city where she was already making friends. A life that was just right for her. She didn't need the Player Prince at her side to make it all complete.

Someone knocked at the door.

Lucy tossed her sketchbook on the bed. It had to be someone in the building—Ed, the super, or maybe Ed's wife, Marie, or Viv. Anyone else would have to ring the buzzer downstairs first. To be on the safe side, she checked the peephole before pulling the door wide.

And her heart stopped dead in her chest at what she saw.

Dami.

Dami in New York. At her door.

Dami, looking like every woman's dream man, tall and dark and so very sexy in that smooth and smoldering way he had—and not only that. So much more than that.

Dami, her friend, who always stepped up when she needed him. The person she most wanted to talk to, to laugh with, to share the snow out the window with, to hold hands with....

Dami.

Oh, God. Dami. For real.

Lucy whipped off the chain, yanked back the security bolt and flung the door wide.

Chapter Ten

The door swung back and Lucy flew at him, calling his name. "Dami!"

He opened his arms and she threw herself at him, jumping up, landing against him with a happy laugh, wrapping her arms and legs around him. She smelled of vanilla and apples and something else, something he'd missed way too much, something that was simply her. "Luce." Her name escaped him in a strange rumble, surprising him with its rawness, sounding like hunger. Like not-so-carefully controlled desire.

Lucy was Lucy, all gushing, gleeful chatter. "Dami, Dami, Dami. I can't believe you're here. I wished and wished you might come. And poof, like a dream. Here you are. It's snowing and it's Christmas. And you came."

"Luce." Heat coiled in his belly, flared across his skin. He was all too aware of the press of her soft breasts to his chest, of those slim legs gripping around him....

And not only that. So much more. He drank in the sight of her, that glowing smile, the sparkle in her soft brown eyes.

Alive, that was it. Lucy was fully engaged, completely alive. Full of light, like her name. She pushed back every shadow, wiped out all cynicism. She made it impossible to be disinterested or disillusioned. She made everything fresh and new.

He should be ashamed, and he knew it, to have agreed to relieve her of her innocence in the first place. And then to have gone ahead and done just that.

And now to be showing up on her doorstep in the burning hope that maybe she would allow him to do it again.

And again.

She tipped her mouth up to him. "Dami..." Breathless. Hopeful. So damned sweet.

He couldn't resist—and who was he fooling? No one. He had no intention of resisting.

He cradled the back of her head, his fingers sliding into her shining silky hair. "Luce." He took her mouth.

She made a soft, yearning little sound as his tongue invaded the warmth and wetness beyond her lips. And then she tightened her arms and legs around him and kissed him back, with no coyness and no hesitation, with complete abandon.

He kissed her harder, deeper, needing the taste of her, needing to fill himself up with the sweetness of her.

And they couldn't go on like this here on the landing. Anyone might wander by.

The door was open behind her. He continued to plunder her mouth as he crossed the threshold with her all wrapped around him, her hands sifting in his hair, her thighs pressing him tight, her kiss as open and eager as her sweet face, her willing heart.

He swung the door shut with his heel. Laughing a little against his mouth, she instructed, "Wait. Back up." He did, and she reached out behind him and engaged the lock. "That way." She kissed the words onto his mouth and pointed over her shoulder down a windowless hallway.

He took her to the bedroom at the front of the apartment. Outside the arched windows that faced the street, snow was falling, thick and steady, reflecting light, filling the room with a silvery glow. The space was crowded with furniture—sewing machines, a wide table, adjustable dressmaker forms. Weaving his way to the bed took some doing, and she didn't help a lot—she was kissing him so hard and deep, moving against him, arousing him, making soft hungry sounds that thoroughly distracted him.

A good thing he was determined. He skirted the second dressmaker form and he was at the bed at last. Easing his fingers under her thighs, he peeled her away from him and gently laid her down.

She stared up at him, softly smiling, eyes wide and so bright, as he undressed her with the ease and swiftness born of years of undressing women. She wore black leggings, a big green sweater that went halfway down her slim thighs and thick socks. He had all that off of her in no time. Underneath, her bra was red lace and her little satin panties were pink. He rolled her over and unhooked the bra and whipped it away.

"Dami…" She rolled onto her back again, laughing a little. Incomparable. Everything about her—the complete lack of pretense or artifice, the small slanted white scars on her rib cage and the longer one, pale as milk, that ran straight down between her breasts. She had no shyness about those scars, no embarrassment. She made them beautiful by her complete acceptance of them.

He bent close, kissed the long one that bisected her above her heart. "You are like no one else I've ever known."

She wrapped her arms around his head, pulled him closer. The scent of her claimed him. "I hope that's good," she whispered.

"It is very good," he replied against her skin.

"Dami." She held him closer. "I have missed you so…."

He clasped her arms and gently peeled them away so that he could straighten and get out of his own clothes. That took even less time than getting rid of hers.

She reached for him again. "Please. Come down to me. Let me hold you."

He grabbed the condoms he'd stuck in a pocket and set them on the nightstand. Then he joined her on the bed.

She wrapped herself around him again. It felt so good, her flesh to his, the scent of her gone musky now, sweeter even than before.

He kissed her some more—starting with her mouth and then moving on, tracing the shape of her jaw with his tongue, trailing his lips down her throat into the warm dip where her collarbones met.

And lower.

He lavished attention on her breasts and her belly, then settled in between her thighs, easing her legs over his shoulders, guiding her knees wider to claim better access. She clutched his head and moaned broken encouragements as he kissed her long and slow and deep. He caressed her with his fingers at the same time, enjoying the feel of her as well as the taste, his mind a hot whirl of excitement and lust for her. At the same time, he remembered to be careful with her, to gauge her readiness. Her body was still new to this, inexperienced, in need of gentle handling.

New but so eager. She was a natural to loving.

It didn't take her long to reach the peak. He felt the quick, hot flutter of her climax against his tongue and she held him tightly to her, crying out, then whispering his name. Her body lifted, bowing up. He stayed with her, kept on kissing her, pressing his tongue at her core, his hands beneath her, cradling her, lifting her closer to his eager mouth.

She shuddered, cried out again and then, with a sigh, went loose. For a little while, he rested his head on her belly and she gently stroked his hair.

In time he rose above her again. Gathering her close to him, he settled her head against his shoulder.

She sighed and whispered, "I want you, Dami...."

"Shh." He kissed her temple.

But she pushed up on an elbow and met his eyes. "I want all of you." Her upper lip was damp with sweat.

He took her face between his hands, pulled her closer and kissed her. "Soon," he said against her mouth. "Shh..." He stroked the short wisps of chestnut hair back from her damp forehead.

"Now," she argued, catching his lower lip between her pretty teeth, biting down a little so that the fine ache of wanting her intensified and he groaned. And then, more firmly, she commanded, "Now."

Who was he to refuse her? Whatever she wanted, he would make sure that she had.

She watched him, her hair a wild tousle of short curls, her eyes low and lazy, looking equally satisfied and determined, as he took one of the condoms from the table by the bed. He had it out of its wrapper and on him in a quick well-practiced series of actions—and carefully, too, so as not to rupture or tear it.

She put her hand to his cheek then, urging him down to her until his mouth settled on hers and they shared another long, sweet kiss.

And what a kiss. She did learn fast. Kissing her now, it was hard to remember how very innocent she had been such a short time ago. This kiss was a woman's kiss, a kiss she took, a kiss she owned. And while she kissed him, she was moving under him, her hands all over him, urging him to cover her.

He gave her what she wanted, burning to have her, impatient as any green kid by then. She made him so hot and needy. She stole his jaded, world-weary nature, gave him back all this urgency, this greed, this heated, hungry tenderness.

He settled above her and she opened to accept him. He tried to go slow, to be careful, be mindful.

But there was no mindfulness for him with her. There was only the welcoming wet heat of her, only her soft hands all over him, pulling him down to her.

Into her.

She took him, she owned him, she moved beneath him and he was the one following, giving back what she gave to him, taking her cues and answering in kind without conscious thought, without calculation. His mind was a whirl of impressions and images. And all of them were of her.

Lucy, too thin, too pale the first time he saw her, running down the steps at her brother's house, her smile blooming in greeting for him, a stranger. Lucy in his arms for a dance that same night, the tip of the scar between her breasts fresher, deep pink. Lucy in her work-room at the house in California, her head bent over a sewing machine, feeding bright fabric under the hum-ming, swift needle....

And Lucy now, beneath him, flushed, sure, powerful.

He gave himself up to her. She took him and she opened him and she turned him inside out.

A little while later he made a quick trip to the loo to dispose of the condom. He returned to her and gath-ered her close and they lay on the bed in the silvery light from the big window, naked, together, watching the snow come down. Her fat orange cat jumped up in the window and watched the snow with them.

He felt content in a way he hadn't for a single day since she left him alone in Montedoro. She was so easy to be with. It had always been that way between them: comfortable. Right. He'd feared that having sex with her would ruin the easiness.

So far it hadn't. Maybe he'd get lucky after all. This new hunger they had for each other would run its course and they would still have their friendship.

God. He hoped so.

He stroked her hair and ran a finger up and down her arm.

She sighed. "That was so good. Oh, Dami, about sex? Seriously, I had no idea what I was missing. And I'm so glad I decided to learn from the best."

He squeezed her shoulder. "No regrets, then?"

"None. And it's not only the sex, Dami. It's...this. You and me, alone, just being together. *This* is so good."

He pressed a kiss against her hair, breathing in the womanly scent of her. "Better than good."

She lifted up enough to look down at him and meet

his eyes. "So tell me. I have to know. How long are you here for? Are you staying upstairs? You weren't wearing a coat, which I'm guessing means you went up to your apartment first.... And what *are* you here for? Business? Where's your bodyguard? When did you get here? Oh, Dami, how I have missed you."

He chuckled. "I missed you, too." *Far too much.* "And do you really expect me to remember all those questions?"

She kissed his shoulder. "Try."

That made him smile. "Fair enough, then. I'll be here through the first part of next week, at least. Yes, I'm staying upstairs. I have some meetings, a project in the works."

"What—?"

He stopped her next question with a finger to her mouth. "Wait until I answer the ones you already asked." She pressed her lips together and nodded in a promise of silence—one he knew she couldn't keep. He said, "Quentin, my bodyguard, is now in his room off my apartment. He's not happy that I refused to let him come down here with me so he could check your rooms for threats."

"Oh, right. I could be planning to kidnap you and hold you for ransom."

"Exactly. You could be a very dangerous woman."

"I could chain you to my bed and never let you go."

He lifted his head long enough to kiss the tip of her nose. "It's an intriguing idea, one we should discuss in depth later."

She put on a shocked expression. "Oh, now I get it. *You're* the one who's dangerous."

"Didn't I warn you about that?"

"You did. I didn't listen—and I'm so glad I didn't."

He caught her chin. "Kiss me." She lowered those soft, warm lips to his in a brushing kiss that ended too soon. He stared up at her and stroked her velvety cheek. "You *are* dangerous," he whispered.

And she giggled. "I guess you needed Quentin here after all."

"No, I didn't. He'd have gone around opening your cabinets and peering in your closets. I didn't want that for our reunion."

She kissed his shoulder. "Our reunion. I like it."

Damien did, too. Far too much. "Where was I? Ah. I arrived here only a little while before I knocked on your door. I went to my apartment, had my driver drop my bags in the foyer and took off my coat while Quentin went up and down the stairs checking for potential threats. Then I sent him to his room and came to find you. Next question?"

"What is the project you're here about?"

"Prepare to be fascinated," he said wryly. "Mass-transit apps."

"Like HopStop? GPS for a subway or bus system, showing you where to get on and get off and change buses to get where you're going?"

"Exactly. We want that for Montedoro. Rule was dealing with it and he had meetings set up here in New York for Monday and Tuesday of next week. But he had a scheduling conflict. I stepped up and volunteered to fill in for him." It sounded perfectly reasonable. But it wasn't the whole truth. He'd wanted to see her again, couldn't stop thinking about her. The transit-app project? Just an excuse.

She kissed him, her hand at his cheek, caressing. "How long will you be here?"

"Until the middle of next week, Wednesday or Thursday...."

"Will you have meetings every day?" She actually blushed. "And yes, I am working you totally, trying to find out how much of your time I can expect to monopolize."

Good. She wanted what he wanted. More of this, the two of them. More time together. More sex. More... everything.

He answered her easily, in a casual tone. "The meetings are scheduled for Monday and Tuesday. I'm hoping to keep them to the mornings both days, but they could go longer...."

"You're free for the weekend, then, and in the evenings?"

"Yes, I am."

"Yay!" She kissed him again, a brush of her lips along his jaw. "Four or five days, you and me. Together." But then she grew tentative. "I mean, if that's good for you. If it's, you know, what you had in mind?"

He clasped her bare shoulder. "It's exactly what I had in mind."

"Oh!" Her smile lit up her face again. "Wonderful."

"What about you? Will you be busy?"

"Well, I did volunteer to make costumes for a children's Christmas show and wrap presents for kids in need. But I can put most of that off until after you leave, so while you're here, I can spend every spare minute with you."

"Excellent." He pulled her closer and never wanted to let go—which of course was ridiculous. He *always* let go in the end. The heat and hunger never lasted, and when it went, his interest went with it. Some men weren't made for forever and he accepted that he was one of those. "We have a plan, then."

"Oh, yeah, we do. A Christmas love affair, the two of us. To go with our Thanksgiving love affair. I could really get used to having love affairs with you."

He stroked her hair and heard himself asking in a casual tone that belied the extent of his interest, "What about that Brandon fellow? Still hoping to make something happen with him?"

"Brandon." She groaned. "Oh, I don't think so. He's not all that after all— Plus, he's in L.A. and likely to stay there. And he's met someone special, he said."

Good. The guy with the butterscotch eyes was out of the picture. Dami smiled against her hair and baldly lied, "Too bad."

"It's okay. Believe me. It's not meant to be with Brandon and I'm totally good with that."

He tipped up her chin, rubbed his mouth across hers, savored her tiny sigh. "About our Christmas love affair?"

She grinned against his lips. "Now you're talkin'."

"Five days is too short." He spoke the bald truth without stopping to think if the bald truth was wise.

She made a happy little sound and tucked her head down on his chest again. "Maybe you'll stay longer, like until New Year's. After all, a Christmas love affair would logically last until New Year's Day, wouldn't it?"

The idea of staying longer held far too much appeal. "Love affairs and logic. I'm not so sure the two go together."

Her lips brushed the side of his throat and her breath flowed across his skin. "I suppose they don't. And I'm sure you have important things you need to be doing in Montedoro, so I'm going to be happy with what I can get. The rest of today and four more days. Maybe five. Too short, but so very sweet."

A little while later they made love again.

And then she cuddled in close to him and chattered away about all she'd been doing since she left him in Montedoro. She talked about her new friend, Tabby, whose family owned the diner across the street. And about the widow in the three-bedroom across the landing. She said that Viviana Nichols made the best cookies in the world.

"I love Viv," she told him. "Her door's always open and she's easy to talk to. It's already beginning to feel like I have a family here, you know? People I really like, good people I want to spend time with."

He wasn't surprised that she made friends so easily. She looked for the good in others and almost always seemed to find it.

Eventually, they shared a quick shower. He would have lingered to make love with her again, but he wanted to take her up to his place. So they put on their clothes and went up to the sixth floor.

"Wow," Lucy said when he ushered her in the door. "I'd forgotten how big it is." He'd brought her up to the apartment briefly when he'd first moved her to New York in October. "All these great windows. An open living space. A real, true New York loft apartment."

"I'm so pleased you approve."

She made a face. "It's just too white, though."

He said what the designer had told him. "Adds to the open effect."

She shook her head, her green sweater drooping off one shoulder, making him want to reach out and slide it down even more—or better yet, to take it off her again. "It needs color. But I do like the art." Large canvases, mostly modern abstracts in the vivid hues she so admired, covered the half walls that marked off the spaces: living, dining, kitchen, all large areas, each one flowing into the next. There were two bedroom suites on that floor—the master suite and a slightly smaller suite. Above, there was another bath, an office and a studio, along with two smaller bedrooms, one for his man, Edgar, when Edgar accompanied him, and one for his bodyguard.

Damien was about to take her up the wide steel staircase and show her the other floor when someone tapped on the door. He checked the peephole. "It's Quentin and the food." He let in the bodyguard and the man with the grocery cart full of meat, staples and produce from a nearby gourmet-food store.

Lucy smiled at the bodyguard, who gave her a respectful nod and then stood to the side so the deliveryman could carry the bags in from the cart and line them up on the kitchen peninsula. Once that was done, Dami signed the bill.

Quentin said, "I'll show you out." He ushered the deliveryman through the door and Dami shut it behind him.

Lucy began pulling things out of the bags. "Yum. Looks good. Is the chef coming soon?"

He came up behind her, drawn as though magnetized to her flesh, to her bright, joyous spirit. Just being near her made him feel electric with energy and heat. He clasped her hips and drew her back against him, lowering his mouth to the sweet-scented curve where her neck met her shoulder. "I *am* the chef."

She turned in his arms and put her hands on his chest. "You can cook, too? I knew it."

"Edgar cooks when I want him to, and brilliantly. But I left him in Montedoro this trip, so I'm on my own."

She stepped out of his hold, scooped up a carton of milk and carried it to the refrigerator. "Come on, Your Highness. Let's put the perishables away."

He watched her move, so light and quick. Desire, stirred by simply touching her, flared higher. He thought what he *shouldn't* be thinking: ways to keep her with him, to keep her close. Ways to have her for as long as he wanted her. Because he'd always been a junkie for sensation and she gave that to him—sensation. Pleasure. Excitement. The burning, false promise of continued delight. In recent years, there hadn't been all that much that gave him the thrill he craved.

But Lucy did. Lucy, of all people. She gave it to him. She made him burn again, made him *care*. Made the world brim with color and happy laughter, with hunger and fire.

He kept reminding himself that she was his friend and he owed it to her to help her get whatever she needed—and what she needed wasn't him. She had shining dreams and ambitious goals. He would only make her forget her dreams, distract her from her goals and leave her wiser in a bad way, hurt and disappointed.

"Dami. The groceries?" She sent him a glowing smile over her shoulder—and he was captured. Enchanted. Completely ensnared.

It was wonderful to feel this way.

His negative thoughts blew away. He decided to stop giving himself a hard time for taking her innocence, for not letting her go when she left him in Montedoro.

She wanted to be with him and he wanted to be right here with her. For now. He was making way too much of this, acting like Alex, his grim, thoughtful twin. He needed to stop that. Introspection, after all, had never been his strong suit.

There was no reason not to take this fine thing between them and go with it. At the moment, it was working for both of them. And who said it had to end badly? Of course he wouldn't hurt her. He would never hurt her.

He reached into the nearest bag and pulled out a crusty loaf of bread and a tub of unsalted butter. As he put them away, he reminded himself that she understood the situation. She had no illusions about him. He'd made it clear that this was no more than a mutually satisfying holiday interlude, that this visit would be a short one.

He only wanted to be with her a little longer. Only four days. Maybe five....

Lucy went down to her apartment later to feed Boris. And then she went back up to Dami's and spent the night in his bed. They made love for hours and it was beautiful. Making love with Dami was about as good as it got. She was so glad she'd chosen him to teach her about sex.

In the morning, she stopped in to check on Boris again and then took Dami over to the diner for breakfast. She introduced him to Tabby, who fanned herself and pretended she might faint when his back was turned. Quentin, the bodyguard, who was lean and sandy haired and mostly expressionless, came with them. He stood near the door, in front of the almost-life-size Virgin Mary and Jesus in the manger, where he could see the entire restaurant and keep Dami in view.

When they left, Lucy hugged Tabby and whispered, "Have a great time with that special guy tonight."

Tabby whispered back, "I will. You, too...."

It was cold outside but clear, with piles of snow left

against the curbs from yesterday. Dami suggested they do the usual Christmas-in-New-York things.

And they did. They went window-shopping on Fifth Avenue and ice-skated at the Rockefeller Center rink. Then his driver took them to Central Park, where they rode on the carousel and strolled the snow-covered paths. It was lovely. And nobody bothered them the whole day. Apparently, the paparazzi didn't know yet that he was in New York. They even stood on the most romantic bridge ever, the cast-iron Bow Bridge over the lake, as the snow started falling again.

Dami kissed her right there on the bridge. His lips were cold at first. But they quickly grew warm. When he lifted his head, the snow caught on his thick black eyelashes.

"Merry Christmas, Dami."

He gave her a slow smile. "Merry Christmas, Luce."

She thought that right then she was as perfectly happy as she'd ever been. She knew it couldn't last and she didn't expect it to. Life wasn't that way. Now and then there was great sweetness and if you were smart, you cherished the sweetness. You held it close and tasted it fully.

But nothing could stay sweet forever. The struggles came. They made you stronger. Even if they never were a whole lot of fun. You cherished the happy times, held them close to your heart to warm you and keep you focused on finding the joy again when things got tough.

That night he took her to a private party at a West Village hotel. They danced and they sat together on a white sofa and drank expensive champagne. He introduced her to the host and to a few other people he did business with in New York. It was all very glamorous and upscale and trendy. A great party, really.

But she had only a few days with Dami. She would have preferred to have been somewhere they could talk without shouting at each other. And then she spotted the photographer taking pictures of them.

Dami saw him, too. He leaned close. "Let's go."

"Great idea."

Quentin appeared with her coat and bag. They were working their way through the crush toward the elevators when she heard a woman's voice behind them. "Damien!"

The woman, tall and gorgeous with platinum hair, emerged from the crowd. She threw her arms around Dami and planted a big one right on his lips.

Dami laughed, a slightly weary sound. "Hello, Susie."

Susie wrapped an arm around his neck. "How long are you in town?"

"A few days. And we were just—"

She shook a French-nailed finger at him. "You know it's been much too long. Let's go somewhere private and talk—or not talk. I can think of any number of interesting ways to pass the time."

"As I was saying, we were just leaving." Dami was no longer smiling. "Let me go."

Susie gripped him tighter. She went further, reaching out her other arm and hooking it around Lucy so she had hold of both of them. "Who's this?"

He repeated flatly, "Let go."

Susie batted her eyelashes Lucy's way. She smelled of expensive perfume and too many drinks. "Aren't you a sweet little thing?"

Lucy gazed back at her patiently. She'd met a few women like Susie. Noah used to date women like her in the years before he found Alice. Beautiful, sexy women who liked to party. A lot.

"Oh, you are just too cute!" Susie hauled Lucy closer and cooed in her ear, "We could have a lot of fun, all three of us."

At which point Dami had had enough.

He reached around Susie and snared Lucy's hand as Quentin moved in behind the blonde, took her shoulders and lifted her neatly out of the way. Dami herded Lucy toward the elevators and Quentin took up the rear, leaving Susie behind.

Dami didn't say a word during the ride back to the apartment building. Lucy kept quiet, too. He seemed pretty upset about the encounter with Susie and she wanted to give him a little time to cool down before trying to talk to him about it.

The driver let them off in front of the building. Dami took her arm then. Her heart lifted a little just to feel his touch. Quentin led the way up the steps and opened the door.

On the elevator, Dami pushed the button for the third floor. Apparently, they were staying at her place tonight. That surprised her a little. His was larger and not chockablock with sewing equipment. But then again, it didn't matter to her where they stayed.

As long as they stayed together.

The elevator stopped. The doors slid wide.

"Hold it," Dami said curtly to Quentin. His brusque tone surprised her. He was never curt, especially not with servants and the people who watched over him. Lucy sent him a questioning glance, but he stared straight ahead as he led her out of the elevator and over to her door.

He turned her to face him then, there in front of her door. His eyes were distant, not really connecting with hers. He brushed a cool hand along the side of her cheek.

Behind him the elevator doors stood open. Quentin waited within, shoulders back, legs wide, expression carefully blank.

"Dami, what—?"

He didn't let her finish. "Good night, Luce."

And then he turned and walked away from her, leaving her standing there staring after him in disbelief.

Chapter Eleven

Damien stepped onto the elevator and turned to find Lucy right behind him.

"Oh, no you don't." She got on beside him.

He gave her his weariest glance. "It's late."

"Oh, stop. It's barely midnight." She reached over and pushed the button for his floor. The doors closed.

He longed to punch the button to open them again. But then what? Scoop her up and carry her bodily back to her door?

And what if she still refused to stay put?

And all right, yes. He was being a jerk. He knew it. He just didn't want to talk about Susie. Leaving Lucy at her door had seemed a way to avoid an uncomfortable conversation.

So much for that.

He maintained absolute silence for the short ride up. Lucy did, too, just as she had during the drive from the party. He found her silence both annoying and unnerving. After all, Lucy was *never* quiet. He'd always thought her incapable of keeping her mouth shut for long.

Apparently, he'd got that wrong.

When the elevator stopped, Quentin exited first. He and Lucy followed, side by side but not touching. Quentin dealt with the alarm, opened the door and went in ahead.

"Thank you, Quentin. That's all for the night."

The bodyguard mounted the stairs for his room above. Damien shut and locked the door.

Lucy set her bag on the entry table and unbuttoned her coat. He took it and hung it, along with his, in the closet by the door. Her dress that night was snug and black, with a lace top that dipped low in back to a V shape. She looked unbearably sweet in it, good enough to eat.

He wanted to kiss her, to run his finger down her back, tracing that V. He wanted to take her straight to bed. However, her level gaze and set expression told him clearly that lovemaking wasn't happening anytime soon.

Then again, maybe he'd get lucky and she'd let him change her mind.

He did what he wanted to do, stepping in close, touching his finger to the nape of her neck, trailing it out along her shoulder to the outer edge of the V. Her skin seemed to beckon him. He needed his mouth on her.

So he took what he needed, kissing the tempting spot where the lace started at the curve of her shoulder while continuing the slow caress with the tip of his finger down to the middle of her smooth back.

She sighed. For a moment, he thought she would melt into his arms.

But then she drew herself up and turned to face him. Her eyes challenged him. "Make me some cocoa, please, Dami."

"Cocoa." He arched a brow, made his expression one of boredom and complete disinterest.

She wasn't buying. "That's what I said. Cocoa, please."

With a curt nod and no expression, he signaled her ahead of him into the kitchen area. She took one of the tall chairs at the peninsula and leaned her chin on her fist as he went through the process of heating the milk and chopping the chocolate.

He thought how he should send her back to her apartment now. He should end this foolishness tonight before it went any further. She was too good, too sweet, too innocent for him. He should tell her he'd been wrong to come here, that he was leaving in the morning.

And then he should check into a hotel, go to those damned meetings Monday and Tuesday and then fly back to Montedoro where he belonged.

As he chopped and stirred, he kept expecting her to start asking him questions.

But again she surprised him. She held her peace until he put the steaming cup in front of her. Then she sipped and said, "So good. Thank you." She set the cup down. "Tell me about Susie."

"That's a bad idea."

"Tell me anyway."

He poured himself a cup and took the chair beside her. "You won't like it."

"Maybe not. But I want to know."

"What, exactly, do you want to know?"

She studied his face for several seconds. He endured

that scrutiny. And then she asked, "How do you know her?"

"You're serious? You actually want to hear about Susie?"

"Didn't I just say so?"

"Luce. I've had conversations like this one with women before. They never go well."

She tipped her head to the side, considering. Then she simply tried again. "I am not *blaming* you. I am not looking for some way to make you the bad guy. I'm only trying to understand who Susie is to you."

"Why do you need to understand that?"

"Because you were going to leave me at my door and walk away in order not to have to talk about it." Damn. Was he that obvious? Apparently, he was. To her. She said, "So I think we need to clear that crap up right now. Tell me about Susie."

"There's nothing to tell. I hardly know her."

"Then this won't take long at all, will it?"

He opened his mouth to give her more evasions— and somehow the simple truth fell out. "I met her at a party very much like the one tonight. It was about three years ago. Here in New York. I think it was in SoHo. She had a girlfriend with her...."

Lucy had her chin on her hand again. "So it was the three of you?"

"That's right. The girlfriend had a loft a few blocks from the party. I spent the night there with them. And the next time I came to New York, I called Susie. There was another girlfriend that time."

"Is that...something you enjoy, Dami? Being with two women at once?"

He felt pinned, grilled. He struck back. "Why? Would you like to try it?"

She picked up her cup again. "I don't think so." Very carefully, she sipped and with equal care set the cup down. And then her sweet mouth trembled. She pressed her lips together to make the trembling stop and asked him hesitantly, "Do I…have this all wrong?"

"What are you talking about?" He growled the words.

Her gaze roamed his face as though seeking a point of entry. A small pained sound escaped her. Finally, she asked, "I mean, should I have let you go, stayed downstairs when you tried to get rid of me?"

All he had to do was say yes—and she would leave him, stop pushing him for answers to uncomfortable questions. But the lie stuck in his throat. "Why didn't you?"

"I told you. It seemed like we really needed to talk this through, so I kept after you. But now… Oh, I don't know. Maybe it wasn't such a good idea to follow you up here. You seem so angry, so defensive. Maybe I'm just butting in where I'm not wanted. Do you want me to go?" She waited for him to speak. When he didn't, she said, "All right, then. I can take a hint." Shifting away, she started to slide down from the chair.

He couldn't bear it. He caught her shoulder. "No." It came out ragged sounding. Raw. "I don't want you to go."

She turned to him again, so many questions in her eyes. "Dami…" She said his name so softly. With tenderness.

He let go of her, knowing he didn't deserve her tenderness. "What?" he asked, low and gruff.

"I'm not judging you." She touched the back of his hand—and too quickly withdrew. He wanted to grab her wrist, to hold on. But he did no such thing. She said,

"I promise you, I am, truly, your friend first of all. I don't want you to be anyone but exactly who you are."

He didn't believe her. "You say that now."

"Because it's the truth. I'm not judging you, but I do want to…understand. I want to understand *you,* Dami."

He felt outclassed. Overmatched. By a homeschooled twenty-three-year-old who'd been a virgin until two weeks ago. He gritted his teeth and confessed, "I've tried a lot of things you might not approve of."

She didn't look the least surprised. "I only wanted to know about Susie because of what happened tonight. For the rest of it, well, Dami, it's your life. I'm happy for whatever you want to share with me, but I really don't need to hear about every single sexual encounter."

"Good."

But she wasn't done yet. "As long as they were with other consenting adults."

He nodded. "They were."

"And no one was injured."

He almost smiled. "No one."

"And, well, now we're on this subject, there's something I should have asked you before, in Montedoro at Thanksgiving, but I was too nervous and afraid I might scare you off and not really planning ahead…"

"Luce."

"Hmm?"

"Go ahead. Ask."

"Do you— Have you always practiced safe sex?"

"Always."

She looked into her cup and then back up at him. "Well. Okay, then." She started to speak—and then didn't.

He commanded, "Tell me. Just say it."

"I… Well, I do care that while you're with me, you're *only* with me. I'm just kind of old-fashioned that way."

The unreality of it—of Lucy as his lover—struck him anew. Never in his wildest dreams would he have imagined himself having this conversation with her. At the same time, after last night and the nights in Montedoro, he couldn't imagine ever wanting anyone *but* her. Which was pure insanity. It might feel stronger with her, *better* somehow. But it was simple sexual attraction and that never lasted. It ran its course and faded, like cut flowers in a crystal vase, like a stubborn head cold.

She spoke again. "If you can't do that, can't agree to be exclusively with me, well, that *is* a deal breaker for me."

He had zero need to think it over. "Of course I can do that." For as long as it lasted, she'd said—which as of now was only until Wednesday or Thursday. And that was yet another absurdity. He couldn't imagine leaving her so soon.

And who did he think he was fooling, anyway? He shouldn't even be here. It would have been better for both of them if he hadn't shown up on her doorstep yesterday, better if he'd never let this thing with them get started.…

"Dami, are you *sure?*"

He didn't flinch, but he wanted to. The question itself was bad enough. Did she have to ask twice? He wanted to be insulted, to lay on the irony: *Well, I might have to grab a quickie with a stranger between meetings on Monday. A man has needs after all.*

But he looked in her eyes and all he saw was sincerity. She was an inexperienced, truehearted woman involved with a man who had no idea how many women he'd had in his bed. Of course she worried that he couldn't be faithful.

So he answered her honestly. "I am sure, yes. Absolutely." He wanted to touch her, to reach for her and draw her close. But that seemed wrong somehow and unfair. He reassured her further. "Until you, I hadn't been with anyone in a while." Not since the last time with V, in August, which had ended in another of her big scenes. "And while we're together, that'll be it. There won't be anyone but you. I promise you that."

She put her hand on his sleeve then. That simple touch hit him deep. It was better by far than any threesome. "I'm so glad."

"It's no hardship. None at all."

She squeezed his arm. "I know you think I'm innocent."

He caught her hand, brought it to his lips. "Because you *are*."

"No."

He kissed the tips of her fingers one by one. "Yes."

She shook her head. "No. Okay, it's true that I haven't had much experience with men. And I like to keep a positive attitude. But still, I'm not innocent, not really. I know what life is. I've been up close and way too personal with death. My dad was dead before I was even born. And my mom…she wasn't right. You know what you said about the powerful love your parents have? Well, my mom loved my dad that way. She never got over that he died. And we lived in this tiny, run-down place and I was always sick and there wasn't any money and Noah wasn't anything like he is today. He was out of control back then, drinking and fighting all the time. And then when I was nine, Mom got sick and *she* died…."

He reminded her gently, "Luce, I know all this."

"I know you do. But what I'm getting at is, when Mom died, I made up my mind that I would be happy no matter what, that whatever suffering or heartache I had to endure, I would focus on the good things. I wouldn't let the losses and the hurts drag me down. I promised myself that I would keep a good attitude. It was not a decision made in innocence. I might have been only nine at the time, but believe me, when my mom died, I hadn't been innocent for years."

He dared to touch her sweet face at last, to trace the graceful arch of each brow, to trail his fingers down her cheek. She made a small questioning sound. And he said, "All right. Not innocent. Good. You are good, good to the deepest part of you. I'm not."

She held his eyes. "Yes, you are." And she laughed a little. "You are very good, I promise you. You are also curious and adventurous and I know you've been wild. So what? I find you generous and helpful, brilliant and fun. Not to mention a truly epic lover."

That did make him smile. "Epic, am I?"

"Legendary. No doubt."

He went ahead and wrapped his fingers around the back of her neck and drew her close enough that he could breathe in the scent of her. "You're just saying that to get me to have sex with you."

She rubbed her soft cheek to his rough one. "Is it working?"

"Truth?"

"Please."

"You had me in the entry when you took off your coat."

A smile bloomed full at last. "Apparently, I'm good in more ways than one."

"And a quick learner, too." He claimed her mouth in a kiss that started out sweet but swiftly turned steamy.

When he let her go, she picked up her cup again and drank the rest. And then she said, "Also, don't forget, I lived in my brother's house for eleven years. And Noah was never a saint. I may not have *done* things until I did them with you, but I know what goes on."

"Noah would hate that you saw more than you should have. His whole life has been about protecting you."

"Dami, get real. Noah likes women. I'm sure you can relate to that."

"Too well, I'm afraid."

"Okay, then. I'm not blind. I saw what was happening. Until Alice, Noah would not give his heart. He didn't want anything permanent and neither did most of the women he hooked up with. And none of that has anything to do with whether or not he protected me. He did protect me. He took excellent care of me and he kept me alive against all odds. That's what matters—and why are you scowling at me?"

"Your brother doesn't want you with me."

She fiddled with her cup and sighed. "That's still bothering you?"

"Think about it. There were paparazzi there tonight. Someone will have gotten pictures of that little scene with Susie. Noah is going to be pissed off when he sees them."

"Too bad. He'll have to look at it as more practice at minding his own business." She got down from the chair and held out her hand to him.

He stood and snared her outstretched fingers, reeling her in and wrapping her in his arms. She tipped up her mouth to him in an offer he couldn't resist. They shared another kiss.

When he lifted his head, she gave him one of those smiles that could light up the darkest night. "So what if Susie made an embarrassing little scene? Too bad if there are pictures online or in the *Enquirer.* And if Noah doesn't like that you're here with me, that's his problem. I only want to know whether or not you're going to let all that ruin the three days we have left."

"You're sure you still want to be with me?" His breath lodged in his throat as he waited for her answer.

She gave it without any hesitation. "Yes, Dami. I'm sure."

Relief poured through him, cool and sweet. And then he frowned. "Wait a minute. *Three* days?"

"That's right."

"How do you get three?"

"Well, it's after midnight, so it's Sunday." She ticked the days off on her fingers. "We have Sunday, Monday and Tuesday. You're leaving Wednesday, so we really can't count Wednesday. That leaves the three days, from Sunday on."

He framed her face between his hands. "I think I should stay until Thursday, at least."

Her eyes were shining. "Four more days." She twined her arms around his neck. "I do like the sound of that."

He bent and scooped her high against his chest. She wrapped her arms around his neck. And he carried her out of the kitchen and straight to bed.

Lucy woke at dawn, snuggled up close in Dami's embrace and thought how right it felt to be there. She burrowed in closer, loving the warmth of him, the smoothness of his skin over all those lovely hard muscles, the absolute manliness of him—and then she remembered Boris.

She kissed Dami's stubbled chin and whispered, "Good morning."

He made a grumbling sound and cupped a hand around the back of her head in a possessive, tender gesture that stole her breath away. "Early. Ugh. Go back to sleep...."

She kissed his chin again. "Can't. I have to go down and feed the cat."

More grumbly noises. His big arms tightened around her. "Stay here. I'll send Quentin to do it."

That made her smile. "There will be scooping involved."

"Quentin can scoop."

"Oh, now. That's just wrong, to send a highly trained bodyguard to clean up after Boris."

"Quentin's a soldier. He's dealt with worse."

"No. *I* have to do it. Boris needs cuddles. He's been alone all night. Don't you even try to tell me that Quentin does cuddles."

Dami ran a hand down her back, tucking her into him even tighter than before. She wanted to stay right there for a lifetime or so. "Promise to make it quick?" he growled in her ear. "Remember, we only have four days left of our Christmas affair."

She laughed at that. "Cuddles take time—but I won't be that long."

Grudgingly, he released her, and then he sat back on the gray satin pillows, laced his fingers behind his head and watched her scurry around naked finding her underwear, her dress—and finally her shoes, one of which had managed to end up halfway down the hall.

"I like that dress," he said, as she wriggled back into it. "I like *all* of your dresses. But I like it even better when you're wearing nothing. I'm thinking I should keep you naked all the time."

"There are so many ways that is totally impractical."

"Allow a man to dream."

She went over and sat on the bed, showing him her back. "Zip me up."

He did, pausing to brush a light kiss below her shoulder blades in the V where the zipper stopped. "I'll walk you out." He breathed the words against her flesh and she wanted to take her dress off again and get back under the covers with him.

But Boris was waiting.

Dami put on his robe and followed her out to the door, where he helped her into her coat. She grabbed her evening bag as he disarmed the alarm.

He kissed her one last time, there on the threshold. "Half an hour, no more," he commanded. "I want you back here with me so we can spend the day in bed together the way we planned."

Downstairs, Boris was waiting for her just inside the door looking very grumpy. She cuddled him, changed his water, cleaned up after him and filled his food bowl with fresh kibble. With ten minutes to spare of the thirty Dami had granted her, she had a quick shower and changed into jeans and a comfy sweater. She was just switching purses when her phone rang.

It was Dami. "You're late."

"I'm on my way. Keep your pants on."

"I'm not wearing any pants."

She laughed, dropped the phone back into her sturdy cross-body bag, pulled open her door—and saw Viviana.

Viv hovered in the open door to her apartment, still in her robe and slippers. She had her hand pressed to her chest. Her face, scarily gray and shiny with sweat, was screwed up tight in a grimace of pain. "Lucy. Hurts…" she barely managed to whisper. Lucy went to her, fumbling in her purse for her phone again as she ran.

Chapter Twelve

Lucy got the 911 dispatcher on the first ring. "Heart attack," she said, almost positive she had it right—and even if she didn't, the two scary words always got the ball rolling.

The dispatcher took it from there, ready with the usual long list of questions. Lucy gave the address and the cross street as she guided Viv down the wall beside the door to her apartment. Viv clutched at her, panting, but Lucy managed to get her seated and supported by the wall with her knees drawn up. The dispatcher asked the questions and Lucy answered, calmly and clearly.

Once the ambulance was on the way—six minutes, tops, the dispatcher promised—the dispatcher had her ask Viv if she was on nitroglycerin.

Viv shook her head and whispered, "No…first time anything like this has happened…."

"She's not on nitroglycerin," Lucy said into the

phone. "She says this is the first time this has happened to her."

Next the dispatcher wanted to know if there was aspirin available. "Chewable, if possible."

Lucy had none. She bit back a groan. At that moment, she almost wished she'd had valve-replacement surgery rather than repair. With an artificial valve, she just might have been on an aspirin regimen and could have whipped a bottle right out of her purse. Then again, she probably would have been on warfarin or...

Dear Lord, what did it matter? The point was she had no aspirin to give Viviana.

She asked Viv, "Do you have any aspirin?"

Viv gestured weakly toward the open door to her apartment. "Master bathroom cabinet..."

Her phone to her ear, Lucy raced inside and down the hall. In the gorgeous retro pink-and-black-tiled bathroom, she found what she needed. "Got them," she told the dispatcher. She grabbed the bottle off the shelf and read the label. "They're the regular kind, not chewable, 325 milligrams."

"Are they timed release, the coated ones?"

"No, the chalky white ones."

"That's better than coated."

"Wonderful. Perfect." Lucy ran back down the hall and out the door to Viv's side again.

The dispatcher gave her more instructions.

Lucy put the phone on speaker, knelt by Viv to set it down on the floor and then shook out one aspirin. She put her arm around Viv. "You need to chew this for thirty seconds before you swallow it. Can you do that for me, Viv?"

Panting, softly moaning, alternately clutching her chest and rubbing her shoulder, Viv managed a nod.

Lucy gave her the pill and counted out the seconds as Viv chewed. It seemed the longest half minute of her life. "All right. Swallow."

Once Viv had the aspirin down, Lucy picked up the phone again. The dispatcher stayed on the line with her, asking questions that Lucy answered as best she could, all the while holding Viv's hand—the one that wasn't tightly clutched to her chest.

After what seemed like forever but was probably no more than the five or six minutes the dispatcher had said it would be, they heard a siren coming on fast, stopping at full volume downstairs in front of the building. Lucy spoke gently, reassuringly, to Viv, who reluctantly let go of her hand so she could step inside the open door to the apartment again and buzz in the paramedics. Endless moments later the elevator doors slid open and two EMTs wheeled their EMS stretcher straight to Viv.

They were just assessing her airway, breathing and circulation and hooking her up to oxygen when Dami came flying down the stairs wearing nothing but a pair of black jeans, with Quentin right behind him.

Dami's face was dead white. "Luce. My God. I heard the siren and I thought…"

She dropped her phone into her purse again, eased around the busy med techs and went to him. "It's not me. Oh, Dami, it's Viv…." He grabbed her against his broad bare chest and she thought how very glad she was to have his arms around her at a time like this.

"What happened?" he asked against her hair.

"She had a heart attack, I think." Lucy looked up at him, drew strength from the simple act of gazing at his dear worried face. "The signs are all there—and I doubt they'll let me ride along in the ambulance with her, but I need to go with her, be with her. Her family's not in New York."

"I'll call for a car."

"Miss." One of the EMTs signaled Lucy. "She's asking for you...."

Dami released her and she went to Viv, who panted out a series of instructions about looking after her place, about getting her little red address book from the drawer beneath the phone and calling her daughters. "And my purse... Insurance card..."

Lucy ran back into the apartment and snatched the large brown shoulder bag from the end of the kitchen counter. One of the EMTs took it from her. She bent close to Viv again and tried to reassure her. "I'm here. I'll take care of all of it, and I'll be following you straight to the hospital...."

"Sweet girl, God bless you...." Viv clutched for her hand again, but the EMTs were already wheeling her toward the open elevator doors.

Lucy called after them, "What hospital?"

One of them told her. They got on the elevator. The doors slid shut. Lucy stared at those doors, suddenly immobilized, images of all the times she'd been the one on the stretcher pounding in strobe-like flashes through her mind.

And then Dami was there, wrapping his big arms around her.

She clung to him. "We have to get going," she said, and then she just stood there, holding him tight, safe in the circle of his embrace.

He pressed his lips to the top of her head. "The car will be here in a few minutes."

"Oh, Dami..." The tears were pushing, trying to get out to turn into a flood that would surely drown her. She bit the inside of her cheek, drawing blood. That did it. The sharp pain brought her back to herself.

He kissed her temple. "Get your coat. Lock up both apartments. I'll run up and put the rest of my clothes on and be right down for you."

Once they were in the limousine and on the way, Lucy called Viv's daughters to break the frightening news.

Marleah burst into tears. Shoshona was calm and thoughtful and then at the end said, "Oh, my sweet Lord. Just let her make it through...."

Lucy told both daughters that Viv had been conscious and still able to talk when they took her away. She promised she would be there until they had her stabilized, all the while sending silent prayers to heaven to match Shoshona's spoken one: *Please, God, let her make it. Let her pull through.* She gave them her number and promised to call them the minute she knew anything more. They both said they would call the hospital right away and be there as soon as they could make arrangements.

When she hung up, Dami reached for her. She unhooked her seat belt, slid across the wide plush seat and settled next to him.

"We're almost there," he promised.

She rested her head on his shoulder and kept on praying that Viv would pull through.

Six hours later they were still sitting in the waiting area outside Cardiac Intensive Care, with Quentin standing guard a few feet away.

A doctor came out to talk to them.

They had Viv stabilized, he said, and the prognosis

was good. They'd put her through the usual endless battery of tests and performed an angioplasty with stent placement. The angioplasty opened the nearly blocked artery that had caused Viv's heart attack, and the stent, a small mesh tube inserted at the same time, would keep the artery open.

Even though she wasn't family, Lucy talked the doctor into letting her go in and visit Viv briefly. As expected, Viv was exhausted and barely conscious. They'd given her a mild sedative to get her through the angioplasty without too much pain. She moved her hand restlessly against the sheet until Lucy settled her own over it, slipping her thumb into the smooth, dry heart of the older woman's palm.

Viv closed her eyes tight. Still, a pair of tears leaked out at the corners and trailed down her temples into her short tightly curled hair.

Lucy bent close and whispered, "You are going to make it. And your daughters are on the way."

Viv let out a tired little sigh at that and managed to give Lucy's hand a weak squeeze. Lucy stayed with her just holding her hand, gently stroking her forehead, until the nurse came in and signaled it was time to go.

A woman came rushing into the waiting area about ten minutes later. She was tall, slim on top and generous through the hips, with honey-colored skin and blond-streaked dark hair. She carried a large shoulder bag and a small suitcase. Lucy liked her style. She wore knee-high black boots, dark tights, a short wool dress and a fabulous heavy coat that reached to midcalf. And especially around the mouth and eyes, she looked a lot like Viv.

Lucy stood up. She had Viv's purse, which they'd given her at the front desk.

The woman spotted her and came right for her. "You have to be Lucy. I'm Shoshona." She dropped the suitcase and they grabbed each other and held on tight.

Lucy tried not to cry, but a tear or two got away from her anyhow. "Your mom's resting now. I know she can't wait to see you...."

Shoshona sniffled a little, too. Then she took Lucy by the shoulders, looked in her eyes for a minute and gave her shoulders a squeeze. "I do believe you saved my mama's life."

"No. I just happened to be there."

"That's what I'm talking about. You were *there* and you did what needed doing and I am so glad. Thank you." She swiped the tears off her cheeks with the back of her hand, which was as slim and beautifully manicured as Viv's.

"I'm just so happy she's pulling through." Lucy held out the purse. "This is your mom's. Her keys are in here, her wallet and cell phone, too— Oh, and there's a small brown bag with her rings."

A nurse appeared. "Mrs. Caudell?"

Shoshona nodded, then asked Lucy, "My suitcase...?"

"We'll look after it," Lucy promised.

"And the purse, too, for now?"

"Of course."

The nurse led Viv's daughter to the long hallway that led into the business end of the CICU.

Lucy took the suitcase and purse back to her chair. She slid them both under the corner table topped with a small artificial Christmas tree. With a long sigh, she sank down beside Dami. He took her hand and folded her fingers over a fresh tissue.

"So much for spending the day in bed, huh?" She

sagged against him and he gathered her in, cradling her in the shelter of his arm, guiding her head down to rest on his shoulder. Again she felt thankful to have him beside her. The awful day would have been ten times worse without the constant comfort of his presence, of his strong arms to hold her when her energy flagged.

"There will be other days," he reminded her softly.

His words warmed her—for a minute. And then she couldn't help thinking that the other days they had together weren't nearly enough.

Tomorrow and the next day, he had meetings. Maybe on Wednesday, which was their last day, they could laze around in bed.

One day for lazing. Uh-uh. No way was it enough.

Yes, Viv was going to make it and she was so grateful.

But why did their Christmas love affair have to fly by so fast?

Two hours later Marleah arrived. Though she was smaller and slimmer than her older sister, anybody could tell the two were related.

Lucy and Dami stayed in their chairs as the sisters shared a private moment. And then Marleah dried her eyes and went in to be with their mom for a while.

When she came back out, Shoshona introduced her to Lucy and Dami.

Marleah recognized him. "Mama's had a heart attack and the Prince of Montedoro is hanging around the waiting room to make sure she's going to be all right."

They all laughed at that, tired laughter. It had been a hard day and it wasn't over yet.

Then Shoshona said to Lucy, "You two go on now. You've been here all day. It's way more than enough."

Dami called for the car and then Lucy asked if maybe one of the two sisters wanted to go back to Viv's place with them. The sisters agreed that Marleah would go. She could take their suitcases, rest for a while and then return to give Shoshona a break.

The drive was a quiet one overall. Marleah seemed deep in thought.

But then, as they approached the apartment building, Marleah shook her head. "This is it," she said with certainty. "Mama can't be living on her own anymore. Denver or Chicago. The day has come when she will have to decide."

Lucy reached over and took Marleah's hand. Marleah didn't object—in fact, she held on tight. "Don't worry about it now," Lucy said softly.

"You're right." Marleah swallowed hard. "But the time has come, oh, yes, it has."

They helped Marleah carry the suitcases up to Viv's place. Quentin put them inside for her.

Lucy hugged her at the door. "I'll be back at the hospital in the morning. Call me if there's anything I can do before then."

"I will," Marleah promised. "You get some rest. Tomorrow, then." She and Dami shared a nod and she went in. Lucy heard her engage the locks.

When she turned back to Dami, he said, "Tired?"

"A little." She went to him, wrapped her arms around his waist and rested her head against his chest. "Life's too scary sometimes."

He stroked her hair. "Your friend will be all right."

She looked up into his waiting eyes. "Yes. I believe that. I know she will."

He kissed her, a light, sweet kiss. "Pack whatever

you need for the night. And we're taking the cat up to my place."

"Good idea." She intended to spend every second she could with him, and the time was flying by way too fast. She didn't want to keep running downstairs to fill Boris's food bowl and give him a hug. The cat could use the company, anyway.

So they collected Boris and all the necessary cat-care equipment and Lucy packed an overnight bag.

They stayed in that night. Dami cooked chicken cacciatore and Lucy had a large glass of wine. He took her to bed early and they made slow, tender love. She woke in the morning to the sound of Boris purring softly from down at the foot of the bed.

Dami came out of the bathroom looking sigh worthy, wearing nothing but a big white Turkish towel. "I've got a breakfast meeting at nine. I'm hoping to be finished by noon, but it could go later. I'll call and let you know."

She wanted to whine at him, to remind him that they had so little time left and he should get those meetings over with and get back to her fast.

But she caught herself. She had him with her only because of those meetings and whining never did anyone any good. She threw back the covers and went to kiss him good-morning.

He and Quentin were gone by a little after eight. She went down to her place to shower and change, stopping to knock on Viv's door on the way out. No answer. The sisters were probably both at the hospital.

She ran into Marie, the super's wife, on the elevator.

"I'm so sorry to hear about Viviana Nichols," Marie said. "I talked to one of her daughters yesterday evening. They say she should pull through all right. I wonder if she'll be moving to be closer to her family. It seems likely, doesn't it, at her age? That's such a nice apartment…."

"I have no idea what Viv's plans are." Lucy gave her a bland smile.

"How's the prince? I didn't realize you two were so…close." The elevator reached the first floor. Lucy got off, Marie right behind.

"Fine," Lucy said. "His Highness is doing fine. And yes, we *are* close. He's a friend of the family."

"But is that *all?*" Marie wanted to know.

"He's been very kind to me." Lucy headed for the door and couldn't resist adding sweetly under her breath, "Last night, he took off all my clothes and was kind to every inch of me."

"What was that, dear?" called Marie.

Lucy gave her a wave and called back, "Merry Christmas, Marie," as she went out the door.

At the hospital, she sat with Marleah and Shoshona. The sisters reported that Viv was holding her own and would be in CICU for another few days at least. After that, if all went well, she would be out of intensive care and into a regular hospital room. If she continued to improve, they hoped that by the weekend she could go home.

The nurses let Lucy go in and visit with Viv briefly.

Viv was awake but still very weak. She whispered in a ragged little voice, "Hello, sweet girl."

Lucy's heart lifted at the words. She pulled up a chair and sat by the bed until the nurse came in and said she had to go.

Dami called her at a little after eleven. His meetings were going late. "It will be after four, I'm afraid, before I can get out of here."

Lucy, in a cab on the way back to the apartment building, tamped down her disappointment and told him that Viv was doing well. "So, um, call me when you're finished?"

"You know I will." And he was gone.

Lucy wanted to cry. Like some big spoiled baby, she wanted to burst into tears because they only had until Thursday and now most of today would be gone before she saw him again. Really, how silly and selfish was that?

She stared out the window at the people rushing by on the street, at the Christmas decorations and window displays, at the Salvation Army bell ringer on the corner and the strange raggedy bearded fellow wearing a dirty fringed rawhide jacket and a coonskin cap. He stopped to throw bills into the bell ringer's bucket.

It was the happiest time of the year. All the Christmas songs said so.

What was there to cry about?

Nothing, she told herself. Not one single thing. Viv was getting better and she would be with Dami that night.

She had the cabbie let her off in front of the Paradise Diner, where she had a bowl of clam chowder and told Tabby about Viv.

Tabby pulled her up out of her seat, hugged her and asked her why she seemed so down. "I mean, she's going to make it, right?"

"Oh, yeah. I'm sure she will. And I'm not down."

Tabby gave her two bags of oyster crackers. "Where's the prince?"

"Working," Lucy grumbled.

"Uh-oh. You've got it bad."

"Oh, I do not. It's not like that."

Tabby frowned. "Like what, exactly?"

"I mean, we're just, you know, having fun...."

"How long's he here for?" Tabby asked way too gently.

Lucy opened one of the little bags and poured the crackers onto her chowder. "Not long enough."

Nestor yelled something in Greek. Tabby turned around and yelled right back at him, also in Greek. Then she muttered, "Why do I put up with him?"

"He makes great clam chowder?" Lucy suggested.

About then, Nestor bellowed, "Order up!"

Tabby waved a dismissing hand in his direction and said to Lucy, "I'm off at two. And I do need to tell you all about Henry...."

"The Saturday-night guy?"

"Oh, yeah." She put her hand against her chest and mimed a fast-beating heart. "He's the one."

Lucy hesitated. She did want to hear about Henry. And she could talk to Tabby. In fact, she might be tempted to start admitting things she hadn't even admitted to herself yet. It would be wiser not to go there.

But who was she kidding? She needed to talk. "Come over to my place. I'll be home."

Lucy made them coffee. They sat in her living room. The view in there was of the wall of the building the next block over, but it was a cozy room, and you could see a little bit of the gray winter sky if you craned toward the window and looked up.

Tabby said she was falling for Henry O'Mara. "Saturday night, Sunday night. He's coming over tonight, too." Her parents weren't happy. They were still after her to patch things up with the nice Greek man she'd almost married. "But *I'm* happy," Tabby said with a giant grin. "Very, very happy in a big, big way." She looked around the room. "Where's the cat?"

"He's up at Dami's. We took him up there last night so I wouldn't have to keep running down here to feed him. We took his litter box, too, which means if I haul him back down here, I need to bring the box. I mean, just in case, right? Ugh. It's complicated."

Tabby laughed. "So get a second litter box."

"It's only for a few days."

"Ah, so that's what's going on with you. The prince is leaving soon and you're missing him already." Tabby sipped her coffee. "Ask him to stay."

"It's not like that. It's not…that kind of a thing between us."

"Do you want it to be *that* kind of a thing?"

Lucy put her hand on her chest. "My heart kind of does. A little." *Liar,* a chiding voice whispered inside her head. *Your heart wants it a lot.* "But he's not a 'staying' kind of guy—or if he was, probably he wouldn't be with me."

"Why not with you?"

"It's just that it's not that way with us."

"What way?"

"We're friends. With benefits, for now. That part— the two of us being lovers, was supposed to be just for Thanksgiving. And now it's only until Thursday. And I'm just starting out, anyway. I'm not ready for anything serious, no matter what my silly heart keeps telling me."

"Shut the front door. Just for *Thanksgiving?*"

"Please. Don't ask me to explain. It's…"

"Do not say 'complicated.'"

"But it *is* complicated."

Tabby set her cup down and leaned toward Lucy. "You need to talk to him about it, tell him how you feel."

"But that's just it. I don't *want* to talk to him about it."

"Yeah, you do."

"No, I want to enjoy the time I have with him and then when it's over, I want us to remain friends."

"But you're *not* enjoying it."

"Yes, I am. Mostly. Mostly, I'm enjoying it a *lot*."

"Lucy, sweetie, you should see your sad little face. Talk to him."

"I feel like such a *child* again. It's the one thing I hate, to feel like a child. I've felt like a child for most of my life, sick all the time, not getting to do any of the things other girls did, with other people hovering, worrying and having to take care of me. And the whole point in the first place with me and Dami being more than friends was for me *not* in any way to feel like a child."

Tabby kicked off her duty shoes and folded her legs up to the side. "Is he treating you bad?"

Lucy gasped. "Dami? Never. Not in any way. And this whole thing, it was my idea. I'm the one who started it, okay? I asked him to be my first lover and he wasn't into it, but as usual, he was a hero about it and tried to let me down easy. But then he discovered that maybe he *could* be into it with me."

"Oh, right. He *discovered* this, did he?"

"No, Tabby. I'm serious. He always thought of me as a kid before, you know?"

"Oh, spare me. I'm a busy woman with my parents' business to run, but even I read the *National Enquirer* now and then. The man is like some world-class lover, right? I'm sure he can tell if he's attracted or he's not."

"Uh-uh. He's not like that, not with me. He's not a player with me. He really has been my friend first and foremost. And we really, truly were just friends until

Thanksgiving. That's when I went after him. I went after him and I kept pushing and finally, well, it happened. We made love and it was beautiful. Exactly what I dreamed it might be. And it's been that way every time since the first time."

Tabby had her lips pursed up and her brow furrowed. "It was supposed to be over after Thanksgiving, you said...."

"That's right. But he had meetings here in New York and, well..."

"What you're saying is *he* started it this time."

"Well, he was here and all, and he lives in the building whenever he's in New York, so of course we—"

"Oh, stop it. He's a prince with buckets of money, right?"

"I don't think I like the way you say that."

"Too bad. The point is, if he didn't want to be with you, he could have stayed at the Four Seasons. You'd have had no idea he was in town. He *wanted* to be with you. *You* want to be with him. It's what I said at the first. You need to talk to him."

"But I told you, this whole thing with him and me was always with the understanding that it was only for a little while."

"And maybe that was your mistake right there."

"What do you mean, my mistake? He's my friend and I trust him and I asked him to do me this very special favor. That's all it was supposed to be."

"So? Now it's more."

"No. You're not listening. I'm honestly not looking for forever right now."

"Oh, honey. Maybe *you're* not. But your heart? That's a whole other story."

* * *

Dami called at four-thirty.

The minute she heard his voice saying he was on the way, Lucy realized what an idiot she'd been. No matter what Tabby thought, she did *not* need to talk to Dami about how she wanted more from this thing between them.

She didn't want more. She was happy with things as they were. Yes, all right, she would be sad when he left. But that was the way it went. That was life. You needed to revel in every moment. You needed to get through the heartache.

And move on.

He took her out to dinner at a great steak house on the Upper East Side and they shared a bottle of very expensive cabernet sauvignon. Lucy ate almost all of her filet mignon—not to mention a prosciutto-and-melon appetizer, cold asparagus salad and a baked potato the size of Long Island. They split a slice of New York cheesecake for dessert.

The restaurant was exclusive enough that no paparazzi popped up to take their picture while they plowed through the huge, delicious meal. They laughed together and toasted Viv's recovery and Tabby's new man and the holiday season in general.

Then he took her back to his place and straight to bed. He made love to her slowly, looking in her eyes. And when he whispered her name at the end, well, she could almost have wished she *did* want forever right now.

Tuesday, like Monday, went by too fast. Lucy went to the hospital in the morning while Dami worked. Again his meetings went on and on. Lucy had time to buy an extra litter box for Boris. Then she went up to Dami's, got the cat and took him back to her place. He kept her company while she worked some more on the detailed sketch of Alice's wedding dress.

They stayed in that night. And in the morning when she woke up, he wasn't in the bed. But she could smell coffee brewing and something delicious cooking.

Breakfast in bed? Did it get any better? They were going to have a perfect day, lazing around without any clothes on, maybe getting up later and doing something festive.

How about a tree for her place? She grinned at the thought. They could get decorations, too. And then they could put up the tree together.

Her grin faded.

And then when he's gone, won't I love that? whined the sad little voice in her head. Every time she looked at the tree she would have to remember this last perfect day, the beautiful time they'd had choosing it and decorating it together.

Uh-uh. Forget the tree. Bad idea. Better just to stay in bed late, make love a lot and go somewhere nice for dinner. And then make love for half the night. That would be a perfect goodbye.

Goodbye. The word seemed to bounce around, echoing, inside her head. Her heart was racing. Her cheeks felt too warm.

She dragged herself up against the pillows and made herself take slow, deep breaths.

She was being an idiot and she was stopping that right now.

Big mistake to start planning out the day. They didn't need a plan. It would be lovely whatever they did.

Her breathing evened out and her pulse stopped galloping. There. She was fine. She wasn't going to break down in front of Dami just because she was beginning to realize she wanted more from him than she'd told him she wanted.

A whole lot more.

You need to talk to him, Tabby had said.

But she wasn't going to talk to him. It wasn't *fair* to put all this emotional crap on him. He hadn't bargained for anything like this.

And neither had she, damn it. Neither had she.

Breathe. Slowly. Deeply.

It worked. Her tight throat loosened. The pressure behind her eyes eased. The heat in her cheeks cooled. It was fine. *She* was fine.

There would be no big scene. She was under control.

And then she looked over and there he was in the doorway, his eyes low and lazy, his mouth made for kissing, wearing a black silk robe exactly like the one he'd worn on Thanksgiving morning when she'd knocked on his door to ask him to teach her about sex. He carried a footed tray with a carafe of steaming coffee, a covered dish of something wonderful and a crystal bud vase with a sprig of mistletoe sticking out of it.

All her deep breathing came to nothing. "Oh, Dami…" She burst into tears.

Chapter Thirteen

Should he have known this would happen?

Of course he damn well should have.

In fact, to be brutally honest, he *had* known it would come to this. Exactly this. And he'd gone ahead and done what he wanted to do anyway.

Damien stood in the doorway, holding the tray with the breakfast she would probably never eat, and cursed himself for being a heartless, lust-driven dog. He shouldn't have come here. He never should have let this thing with them get started in the first place.

She was his friend, dear to him. She deserved so much—everything.

Instead he'd had to go and become her lover when he knew himself and knew how it would end: just like this. With her suffering and him hating himself.

He set down the tray and went to her. "Luce, my darling…"

She had her head in her hands. Her slim shoulders were shaking. He reached for her and she sagged against him with a lost little sob.

He gathered her closer, stroked her soft hair. "Shh…" He knew the words to say, the gentle reassurances. "It's all right. Don't cry. Everything will work out…."

"Oh, no." A gasp, another sob. "I don't think so." He felt the warmth of her tears against his throat.

He cradled her face, tipped it up to him, wiped at her tears with his thumbs. Her eyes glittered, wet. Yearning. Her mouth trembled and he wanted to kiss her, to taste the salt and the wet, to pull the covers away and make love to her again.

One more time. Before he left.

He didn't do what he wanted. For once.

Her eyes sought something in his face. He doubted she found it. She said, "Dami, I've been lying. Lying to you. Lying to *me*. I thought I could do it. Could just keep on lying until after you'd gone."

He did kiss her then. But he kept the kiss chaste, though her mouth trembled, willing, beneath his.

When he lifted his head, he saw she was on to him. "Kisses can't keep me from saying it," she whispered.

"Luce…" It was a warning. And a plea.

She said it anyway. "I love you, Dami. I'm *in* love with you."

There. She'd gone and done it. Said the three words that couldn't be unsaid. The ones that always made him feel restless, eager to be gone.

And she wasn't finished. "I think I've been in love with you since that first night I met you, when you danced with me and treated me with such complete consideration. You talked to me, *really* talked to me, and you listened, like you really were interested in me and what I had to say, as though I was more than some sickly, scarred-up, skinny girl. Like I was a grown woman, beautiful and whole and strong and well."

"That was exactly how I saw you."

Through her tears, she gave him a certain look. Knowing. Patient. "As a grown woman? Hardly. You saw me as a child, Dami. You might even have loved me, too—as a friend, I mean. Or at least felt affection for me right from the first. I knew that you did. I felt that you liked me. I knew you *noticed* me. And you were kind to treat me as a grown woman when you knew how I longed to be thought of as a fully functioning adult. But you didn't *see* me as a woman. Not then. Don't try to tell me that you did."

He gave it up. "All right. As a child. I thought of you as childlike. And I adored you from the first."

"Okay," she said halfheartedly. "I'll buy that." She swiped at her eyes with the back of her hand. He grabbed the box of tissues from the nightstand and offered it. She took it, pulled one out, dropped the box on the bed. "You liked me and I *loved* you. I just didn't realize the *way* that I loved you."

"Luce. It doesn't matter."

"But I've been dishonest, in my heart."

He shook his head. "I don't care."

She gasped. "But I…I used our friendship to get you to make love with me."

"Yes, you did. I knew that from the first. You did nothing wrong."

Her soft mouth twisted. "Why don't you get it?"

"But, Luce, I do get it."

"Uh-uh. No. All along I've been telling myself that it was just for Thanksgiving, just for these past few days, just for a little while, for *experience* so I could get some

guy like Brandon to look twice at me. I've been telling myself that I didn't want anything permanent, that
I only wanted a few lessons in love and then we would
go back to being like we were before. That was a lie.
A lie, do you hear me? All along, deep down where it
matters, in the heart of me where the truth is, I've been
hoping, praying, longing for you to fall in love with me.
I've been wanting a chance at forever with you."

He took her hand. She allowed that, which surprised
him a little. Her fingers felt cool and smooth in his. He
kissed them. "I lied to you, too."

"No." She looked as though she might cry again,
those big eyes filling. With the tissue in her free hand,
she dashed the tears away.

He confessed. "I came here on Friday because I
wanted to see you again, to be with you again. When
Rule couldn't make it for the transit-app meetings, I
jumped at the chance to fill in for him."

Hope lit her wonderful face from within. "You…you
wanted to be with me, too?"

"Of course I did. I *do,* but…"

She saw the truth in his eyes and pulled her hand
free of his. Bleakly, she said the rest for him. "Not in
a forever way."

"That's right."

Dipping her head, she stared at the tissue between
her hands. "So if not in a forever way, what kind of
way, exactly?"

He'd thought he'd hated it when she cried. This was
worse. But she was Luce and even if he was incapable
of giving her the love she deserved, he still adored her,
and she wanted the truth now. What else was there to
do but lay it out there for her? "You excite me, Luce.
From the minute I started to see you as a woman, from

that first kiss by the harbor on Thanksgiving Day, I've wanted you. I seem to have developed a real obsession with you. It keeps getting stronger. I know I should leave you alone, but I, well, I know you want me, too. I couldn't stop thinking about you, wanting you. So I came here to you. For more."

She looked at him sideways and licked her lips, sending a bolt of lust straight to his groin. God, he was hopeless. She asked, "But it's just sex with you, that's what you're saying?"

He nodded. "And I do like you."

"Like. You *like* me." She seemed to be testing the words, turning them over in her mind.

He'd never in his life felt so completely inadequate. "Is that so bad? That I like you?"

"Not…love? Not the forever kind of man-and-woman love?"

"No. Not that."

"But…could it grow into love? Is that possible?"

"God, Luce. What do you want from me? You know how I am. I told you. I've seen the kind of love you're talking about. My parents have it. Most of my brothers and sisters have it. I understand myself well enough to accept that I don't have the attention span for that kind of love."

She tipped her head to the other side and she looked him up and down in a measuring way that made him want to grab her and pull her under him and bury himself in the welcoming wet heat of her. "But you want me? You *still* want me, even after what I said about loving you, about lying to myself about loving you. You want me right now. You want to grab me and kiss me and do all those things to me that make both of us happy, that make both of us burn."

He readjusted his robe, though he knew she'd already spotted the evidence that she had it right. "What are you getting at?"

She canted marginally closer. The scent of her drifted to him, unbearably womanly, so damn sweet. "You want me."

He gritted his teeth. "You keep saying that."

"But only because *you* keep saying it. Because I can see it in your face every time you look at me." She licked her lips again. Why did she keep doing that?

"What the hell?" He jumped to his feet and glared down at her. "What are you doing? What's going on here?"

She stared up at him. Proud now. Defiant somehow. "I'm not sure I can have children, Dami. I'm not sure it would be safe. Pregnancy puts a big burden on the heart and the circulatory system. I would have to consult with my doctors, assess the risks."

"Risks?" Now she was scaring him. "Children?" He backed away from her, from the bed. "What do children have to do with anything?"

"Nothing." Her eyes filled again. She blinked those tears away. "I just, well, I wanted you to know. I want you to know everything. All the truths that are so hard to say."

"Why?"

She closed her eyes, looked away. But then she straightened her shoulders and faced him again. "Because you are my hero, Dami. You're the one who danced with me and treated me like a woman when no one else could. You're the one who encouraged me to follow my dream. And then when Noah wouldn't let me go, you're the one who came and got me, the one who freed me, the one who brought me here to New York where I needed to be. You're the one who sat with me all day Sunday in the hospital, making the fear and the worry bearable for me, because I had to be there for Viv. You're the one who taught me the magic that can be between a woman and a man. You showed me... everything. And everything that you showed me has been so very beautiful. That's why I want, why I *need,* to tell you the truth. That's why I love you, am *in* love with you. How in the world could it be any other way for me?"

He felt shame then, a twisting, sour sensation deep in his gut. "I'm not. Not all that."

"Oh, Dami. You are. And I hope, I pray, that some-day you will see that you are." She pushed back the covers. Naked, glorious, she swung her slim legs over the edge of the bed and stood.

He feared she would come to him, touch him, lift her mouth to him. If she did, he would take her, make love to her now. And that would be another wrong to add to all the rest of it. "What are you after?" He growled the words at her.

She faced him, so beautiful in the gray light of that December morning. Naked and self-contained, her eyes dry now. "I'm going to get my things together and go back to my place."

"Right now. Just like that?"

"Just like that."

He wanted to argue with her, to shout at her that they weren't finished here. But why tell more lies? He might not be ready to let her go yet. But that didn't mean it was any less over. He couldn't give her what she needed, what a woman like her deserved.

The least he could do was to let her walk away now that she was ready to leave him.

"Suit yourself." He went over and poured himself some coffee from the carafe on the tray. Then he dropped into the chair there and sipped slowly as she put on her clothes and gathered up the few things she'd left around the apartment.

In no time, she stood before him, her overnight bag and purse on her shoulder, the fat orange cat under one arm. "Can you just send Quentin down with the litter box and food and water bowls and anything else I've forgotten to take?"

He set down the empty coffee cup and considered maybe begging her not to go.

A hero, she'd called him. She had it all wrong.

He said, "Of course I'll send Quentin down."

"Merry Christmas, Dami." And that was it. The end.

He watched her until she went through the door and disappeared from his sight down the hall.

Chapter Fourteen

Montedoro was beautiful at Christmas. This year, the beautification committee put up a forest of brightly lit trees in a rainbow of colors around the casino and the Triangle d'Or. As always, all the staterooms of the palace were decorated, each with its own Christmas tree, with swags and lights on every banister and mantel.

There were parades and special Christmas markets, and an endless round of gala celebrations. Damien went to the market as was expected. He attended the parties. At the Christmas Ball, he danced with his mother and sisters and sisters-in-law.

He went through the motions required of him. He smiled. He chatted. He held up his end. If anyone noticed his heart wasn't in it, they had the good sense to keep their observations to themselves.

Noah surprised him with a call on Christmas Eve.

"Merry Christmas, Dami. I saw the pictures of you and Lucy and that hot blonde. Didn't like seeing those."

What could he say? "It was embarrassing. I should have handled it better, seen Susie coming."

"Her name is Susie, huh?"

"We all have regrets, Noah," he answered flatly. "Things we should have done better. Things we probably shouldn't have done at all."

"Hey. I hear you there." And then Noah actually laughed. "I talked to Lucy about those pictures. She told me—again—to stay out of her business. I'm trying to do that. She says I'm getting better. Alice says so, too. I'm telling myself that's progress." A pause, then, "Lucy says you're not seeing each other anymore."

He felt a definite twinge somewhere deep in his chest. "That's right."

"That's too bad. I was kind of getting used to the idea of the two of you together."

He really didn't want to talk about it. He said nothing. Maybe Noah would take a hint.

No such luck. "Alice says…" Noah let his voice trail off, leading him on.

And Dami took the bait, demanding bleakly, "Alice says what?"

"That you're in love with my sister and that Lucy loves you back. That the two of you have been in love almost since you met—it just took you both a couple of years to figure it out."

Dami had no idea what to say to that.

Noah spoke again. "I make it a point to listen to Alice. She's usually right."

"Noah." It came out loud and very aggressive. He lowered his voice with effort. "It's over." He was not, under any circumstances, going to ask about her. But then, of course, he did. "How's she doing?"

"Okay, as far as I can tell. Celebrating Christmas with her new friends. That would be Tabby from Lucy's favorite diner and Tabby's new boyfriend, whose name is Henry, and the older woman on Lucy's floor in your building, the one recovering from a heart attack."

He'd been wondering about Mrs. Nichols even though he'd never actually met the woman face-to-face. "Viviana's her name. She's getting better, you said?"

"She's doing well. And she's at home now. One of her daughters is staying with her. After New Year's she's moving to Chicago, I think Lucy said. Lucy said her neighbor is very independent, but she also understands that the time has come when she needs to live near her family."

"Luce will miss her."

"I think she's already making plans for a visit to Chicago."

Damien made a low sound that could have meant anything and then kept his mouth shut. Better to leave it alone, stop talking about her.

When the silence stretched out, Noah said, "Well, I only called to wish you happy holidays. Alice sends her love."

"Take good care of my sister."

"I will— And, Dami?"

"What?"

"You're an idiot, you know that?"

He didn't even bother to get angry. There was nothing to be angry about. It was only the truth on a whole lot of levels. "Happy holidays, Noah." And that was that.

Christmas morning he had breakfast in his parents'

private apartments. Five of his siblings were there, along with their spouses and children. It was a happy time. They ate and opened the gifts piled high under the fifteen-foot Christmas tree, set up as always in the curve of the stairway by the door.

Around noon, on his own, he took several small brightly wrapped packages and walked to the café in La Cacheron where he'd taken Lucy at Thanksgiving. The café was always open on Christmas Day from nine to two. Regular customers appreciated being able to get their croissants and beignets fresh even on the holiday. The walk was a pleasant one and he didn't spot a single paparazzo. Apparently, even the tabloid vultures took a little time off for Christmas.

The café was quiet when he got there, with only two customers, one at the counter and another at a table by himself in the center of the room. Dami took a corner seat and put the presents on the table. Justine served him his usual coffee and pastry. She chose a gift and smiled a thank-you. One by one the others came by. Each took a gift and thanked him. They all knew what was inside. He gave them all the same Christmas tip every year, each one tucked in a small box and wrapped in bright paper tied with a shiny bow.

He was sipping the last of his coffee when the door opened and in strode Vesuvia. Before he had time to do anything but wish himself elsewhere, she spotted him and stalked over like a lioness on the hunt.

"There you are." She posed with her nose in the air, one hand on the back of the bentwood chair across from him. "I knew you would be here."

"Come on, V. Let's not do this again. I'm through, you're through. It's over, long over. And we both know it."

She yanked back the chair and flung herself into it.

"This is ridiculous." At least she was whispering. And the café remained nearly empty. It was just possible he could get rid of her without too much of a scene. She added, "I know that you and the tacky little wannabe fashion designer are through."

Fury blasted through him. "Do not speak of her," he said, very softly. And how did she know that he and Lucy were through? Better not to ask.

V sneered, "She doesn't matter, anyway."

He smacked his fist on the table. His cup, spoon and plate jumped.

Vesuvia's sculpted nostrils flared. But when she spoke again, still whispering, she had the sense to leave Lucy out of it. "You must stop being so stubborn. I want to get moving on our wedding plans. It's going to be the wedding of the decade, Dami. And as of now, we have only a year to put it together."

"There isn't going to be any wedding," he said.

For all the good that did. "Have you forgotten that you'll be thirty-two in exactly a month? Next year will fly by. And then what? You'll be thirty-three. Have you suddenly forgotten the Marriage Law?"

"I don't care about the Marriage Law."

"Of course you do." She swore softly in Italian. "If you don't marry soon, you'll lose your inheritance and your titles, too. You'll no longer be a prince of Monte-doro."

"How many ways can I say it? I'm not marrying you, V. It's long over with us. When are you going to accept that and move on?"

She rolled her eyes and asked in a smug whisper, "Why should I accept it? You need me. You need to marry and I want to marry you. It's all going to work out. You only have to stop denying the inevitable."

He shook his head. "No."

She stuck out her chin at him. "Don't tell me no. I understand you. I know how you are. Yes, I have a temper. Yes, I am sometimes unreasonable. But in the end, I'm willing to forgive you, whatever you do. I will forgive you and we can move on. We both know how you are, Dami—born to stray." He felt more than a little insulted. All right, he was no model of virtue, but he'd been faithful to V. It had mattered to him to be true to the woman he intended to marry. Even when they'd been on the outs, she'd been the only one in his bed until after it was undeniably over. Until Thanksgiving. Until Lucy. V sneered, "With you, Dami, there will always be someone new, and you will require a forgiving wife."

And by then he'd had enough. "You have no idea what I require."

"Yes, I do, I—"

"No. No, you don't. I require love," he said, and it was true. "I want forever, with the right woman."

Vesuvia sighed heavily and tossed her hair. "Oh, please."

"I want forever with Lucy Cordell."

There was a moment. Huge. Endless. Vesuvia gaped at him. He stared back at her. He hadn't planned to say it, hadn't even known he *would* say it until the words were on their way out his mouth.

But now he'd done it, now he'd let himself say it, the stark, simple truth in it stunned him.

V whispered dazedly, "You can't be serious."

"I am completely serious," he replied. "I'm in love with Lucy Cordell and I have been for a long time now. There's no one else for me. Lucy's the one."

* * *

On Christmas night, Lucy gave a little party at her place. Tabby came with Henry after taking him to her parents' house for an early dinner first.

"It could have been worse," she told Lucy. "At least they didn't yell. No heavy objects were thrown. I think we're making progress."

Shoshona and her husband, Tony, were staying with Viv until January, when they would take Viv back to Chicago to live. All three came to the party. Viv even brought frosted Christmas cookies that she and Shoshona had made together.

A couple who lived on the fifth floor, Bob and Andrew, came, too. Lucy also invited two new friends in their mid-twenties. Sandra and Jim were actors Lucy had met while making Christmas-show costumes for the Make-Believe and Magic Children's Theatre Company.

It went well, Lucy thought. She served drinks and snacks and they played a game called Cranium that Bob and Andrew brought along. Everyone seemed to have a good time. They all stayed until well after midnight.

Sandra was the last to go. She offered to stay and help clean up. But Lucy hugged her and shooed her out the door. She would deal with the mess in the morning.

She took Boris and went to bed. As usual, since Dami had left her, sleep didn't come easy. She missed making love with him, but she missed his big body wrapped around her in sleep even more.

That didn't make a lot of sense, and she knew it. They'd been lovers for such a short time. Two nights in November, five in December. It was nothing. A blink of an eye, really.

And yet for her it didn't seem to matter how few the

nights had been. Her bed felt too big and too empty without him.

In the morning, the sun was shining, making the snow on the windowsills glitter like sequins on a white party dress. She plugged in her tree lights, made herself breakfast and counted her blessings. After a second cup of coffee, she started gathering up the dirty glassware and dishes from the night before.

When the doorbell rang, she assumed it had to be Bob or Andrew. They'd left the Cranium game behind last night. She grabbed the game from the coffee table and carried it to the door, disengaging the locks and pulling it open without even stopping to check the peephole.

Dami stood on the other side.

A strange, incoherent little sound escaped her at the sight of him. She gaped at him, not believing, certain she had to be seeing things, that she'd missed him so much she'd gone delusional.

Dear Lord, he looked good. It wasn't fair that he looked so good. He wore a fabulous camel coat over one of those perfectly tailored designer suits of his. His dark eyes locked on hers and something inside of her went all wimpy and quivering. "Hello, Luce."

She almost dropped the Cranium game. But then by some miracle, she managed to hold on to it. She backed up without speaking, clearing the doorway.

He came in, bringing with him the wonderful, subtle scent of his cologne and a bracing coolness in the air. He must have come up straight from outside.

She gulped as he shut the door. "Uh. Where's your bodyguard?"

"I sent him on to the apartment."

"Oh. Well." Her mind seemed filled with cotton, her

thoughts not connecting properly. At the same time, her whole body ached. She wanted to launch herself at him, grab on tight and never let go. But no way was she doing that.

Okay, he might really be standing in front of her after all. But his presence didn't mean he'd come for her. He could be in New York for any number of reasons.

"Have a seat." She set the game on a side table and gestured in the general direction of a chair.

He stayed where he was. "God. Luce." He said it low. Soft and rough at the same time. As if he really had missed her. As if his arms ached to reach for her.

Or maybe that was only wishful thinking on her part. "What are you doing here?"

He stuck his hands in the pockets of his beautiful coat. He looked down at his Italian shoes, then lifted his head again and locked those amazing dark eyes on her. There was pain in those eyes. And hope, too. And longing. Wasn't there?

She didn't dare to believe.

But then he spoke. "I was wrong. So wrong. I didn't know, not really. I didn't let myself see. I'd convinced myself it wasn't going to happen for me, that somewhere along the line, between one barely remembered liaison and the next, I'd lost whatever it takes, that willingness of the heart. I'd lost whatever chance I had of finding a woman to love, a woman I could love with everything in me, the way my father loves my mother. But then I met you."

She put up a hand, palm out. "I don't understand. You said you couldn't love me...."

"Luce. I was wrong. You're the one. The only one for me. I'm here because I had to come, to take a chance that maybe you might forgive me for being such a complete ass, for turning you down, for not seeing the truth sooner, for not letting you show me what you've been trying to show me. I'm hoping, I'm praying that just maybe it's not too late."

Tears scalded the back of her throat. She gulped them down. "But how? When…?" Her throat clutched and she couldn't finish.

"Yesterday," he said. "Christmas Day. I was at my favorite café in La Cacheron. You remember the one?"

"I remember, yes."

His eyes went bleak. "Vesuvia cornered me there. She started in on me about how I was going to have to marry her."

"Because of the Marriage Law, you mean?"

"That's right. She started laying out all the reasons why she was the right wife for me. She said she understood me, she knew what I required in a wife. And then, out of nowhere, shocking the hell out of both of us, I just said it. I said it out loud without even stopping to think about it."

"Said what?"

"That what I require is love and forever. That I'm in love with *you*. That you're the only one I would ever marry, the only woman for me."

The chains of hurt around her heart loosened. The sunny day seemed brighter still. Could this really be happening? Could all of her dreams, every last shining one of them, miraculously come true? "I don't… Dami, what are you saying? Are you asking me to marry you?"

He raked a hand back through that thick midnight hair. "I know you're young. I know it's probably too soon to be talking about marriage. I was just telling you what I said to Vesuvia, which was only the simple, absolute truth. I love you, Lucy Cordell. I want only you. I want us to have a life together. I've been thinking about how we might make that happen. I know your dream is to go to school here. So if you would have me, if you would give me another chance to show you all you mean to me, I would make New York my home base. I would move in upstairs. *We* would move in upstairs. You could keep this place, if you want it, for your work. Or whatever...."

Her silly mouth kept trembling and the happy tears wouldn't stay down. "Oh, Dami. I can't... I don't..." She had a million questions. She asked the first one that popped into her head. "But what about the Marriage Law? Don't you *have* to marry someone soon?"

He smiled then, at last, that wonderful, unforgettable killer smile of his. "Yes, if I don't marry within a year of my next birthday, I lose my titles and all I've inherited as a prince of Montedoro. But I do have three brothers ahead of me in line for the throne. And all three of them have children. And after me there are five sisters. The Bravo-Calabrettis will have no problem holding the throne whether I remain a prince or not. And my inheritance aside, I've done well for myself. I don't *have* to marry anyone to continue living in the style to which I've always been accustomed."

"So that's what you meant at Thanksgiving when you said you were going to leave it alone, not worry about the Marriage Law anymore."

"Exactly."

"And so...you *don't* want to marry me?"

He laughed. "Of course I want to marry you." He grew serious again. "I just think you need more time to deal with that. And I'm willing to give you as long as you need."

"Oh, Dami..."

"Whenever you're ready, say the word. We'll get married tomorrow if that's what you want."

"You mean that?"

"I do. With all of my heart."

"Is this…a dream? Am I still asleep?"

"No dream, Luce. Real. You and me forever. That's what I want. I found you—and then I lost you through my own blind pigheadedness. If you'll only take me back, I will always be here for you, always love you. *Always,* Luce. I swear it."

She didn't want to break the spell of all this wonderfulness with her deepest fear. But she knew that she had to. "I only… What about the children? What if I can't have your children?"

His gaze never wavered. "You're the one for me. That's what matters. We'll deal with the challenges as they come. If we never have children or if we adopt or find a surrogate… Whatever happens, as long as you're with me, as long as we can face it together, we can get through it. We'll be all right."

"You sound so certain."

"I *am* certain. I was an idiot. Your brother even told me so. But not anymore. Never again."

"Noah said you were an idiot?"

"Yes. He called me on Christmas Eve. He said I was an idiot to leave you. He was right. Luce, I know what I want now. I get it at last. I am absolutely sure that you are the one for me. The question is, what do *you* want?"

"Oh, Dami…"

He watched her, waiting for her answer. His eyes were so bright, full of hope. Full of yearning.

She saw the truth in him then, and she believed. His heart was hers to take.

"Yes," she answered with total conviction. "You're

the one for me, too. Oh, Dami, there's no one else, there never could be. I love you so much."

"Luce." He opened his arms to her.

She ran to him. He grabbed her close.

The kiss they shared made her head spin and her knees go weak. He was her friend, her prince, her hero, her hot and tender holiday lover. And now, at last, on the day after Christmas, he was giving her the gift she wanted most of all. That gift was his love.

She had his heart and he had hers. Forever belonged to the two of them now. They would claim it hand in hand, together.

* * * * *

Watch for Max and Lani's story,
THE PRINCE'S CINDERELLA BRIDE,
coming in May 2014,
only from Harlequin Special Edition.

#2305 HAPPY NEW YEAR, BABY FORTUNE!
The Fortunes of Texas: Welcome to Horseback Hollow
Leanne Banks

Refusing to be burned again by love, single mom Stacey Fortune Jones avoids romance at all costs. But when bachelor cowboy Colton Foster charms his way into her heart, she just might rethink her attitude toward what he has to offer....

#2306 MATCHED BY MOONLIGHT
Bride Mountain • Gina Wilkins

Innkeeper Kinley Carmichael meticulously plans every part of her life. As travel writer Dan Phelan, who's leery of anyone so intense, helps Kinley let her hair down, he finds that he can't resist this lovely woman who's just walked into his life....

#2307 IT BEGAN WITH A CRUSH
The Cherry Sisters • Lilian Darcy

In high school, good girl Mary Jane Cherry fell hard for golden-boy jerk Joe "Cap" Capelli. When they meet years later, Mary Jane wants to believe Cap has changed, but is reluctant to trust him. She's about to find out that time heals all wounds—and might just create true love!

#2308 THE SHERIFF'S SECOND CHANCE
Michelle Celmer

When teen sweethearts Cait Cavanaugh and Nate Jefferies reunite, sexual tension still simmers between them. But Cait pushes single dad Nate away, despite her feelings for him. Will this high school romance remain in the past, or can it have a real future?

#2309 REID'S RUNAWAY BRIDE
The Colorado Fosters • Tracy Madison

Daisy Lennox left Reid Foster at the altar on their wedding day when she discovered a terrible secret. Eight years later, Daisy is back in Steamboat Springs, but Reid still wants their happily-ever-after. Will this Colorado prince win over his footloose ex-fiancée?

#2310 THE DASHING DOC NEXT DOOR
Sweet Springs, Texas • Helen R. Myers

City girl Brooke Bellamy comes to Sweet Springs, Texas, to care for her ailing aunt Marsha. Her neighbor, hunky veterinarian Gage Sullivan, captures her heart—and her aunt's basset hound—but can Brooke leave the corporate world behind to find a forever family?

YOU CAN FIND MORE INFORMATION ON UPCOMING HARLEQUIN® TITLES, FREE EXCERPTS AND MORE AT WWW.HARLEQUIN.COM.

HSECNM1213

SPECIAL EXCERPT FROM

H HARLEQUIN

SPECIAL EDITION

*Romance is the last thing on new mother
Stacey Fortune Jones's mind…until rancher Colton Foster
comes along. Will love emerge where she least expects it?*

***

"What are you thinking?" he asked.

She told herself to get over her self-consciousness. After all, this was Colton. He might as well be one of her brothers. "If you must know, Mr. Nosy, I was thinking that you have the longest eyelashes I've ever seen on a man. A lot of women would give their eyeteeth for your eyelashes."

Surprise flashed through his eyes and he laughed. It was a strong, masculine, happy sound that made her smile. "That's a first."

"No one else has ever told you that?" she asked, and narrowed her eyes in disbelief. Although Colton wasn't one to talk about his romantic life, she knew he'd spent time with more than a woman or two.

He shrugged. "The ladies usually give me other kinds of compliments," he said in a low voice.

Surprise and something else rushed through Stacey. She had never thought of Colton in those terms, and she wasn't now, she told herself. "What kinds of compliments?" she couldn't resist asking.

"Oh, this and that."

Another nonanswer, she thought, her curiosity piqued

The song drew to a close and the bandleader tapped on his

microphone. "Ladies and gentlemen, we have less than a minute left to this year. It's time for the countdown."

Stacey absently accepted a noisemaker from a server and looked around for her daughter. "I wonder if Piper is still with Mama," she murmured, and then caught sight of her mother holding a noisemaker for the baby.

"Five…four…three…two…one," the bandleader said. "Happy New Year!"

Stacey met Colton's gaze while many couples kissed to welcome the New Year, and she felt a twist of self-consciousness. Maybe a hug would do.

Colton gave a shrug. "May as well join the crowd," he said, and lowered his head and kissed her. The sensation of the kiss sent a ripple of electricity throughout her body.

What in the world? she thought, staring up at him as he met her gaze.

"Happy New Year, Stacey."

***

Enjoy this sneak peek from
USA TODAY bestselling author Leanne Banks's
HAPPY NEW YEAR, BABY FORTUNE!,
the first book in
The Fortunes of Texas: Welcome to Horseback Hollow,
a brand-new six-book continuity
launching in January 2014!